A Quiet Holiday

Roxanne Mercier

Contents

Prologue

Sienna

There are many things in this world that can make you feel insufferably alone at times.

Witnessing happy couples when you've not long broken up with someone, and that break-up was not your choice, definitely slots right into that category.

At the moment, however, I am experiencing a whole new horrendous twist on that particular type of torture.

I'm trying so hard to concentrate on the book I'm reading, but my furious gaze keeps being drawn again and again to the couple on the other side of the pool.

They can't keep their hands off each other, and are trying to share one sun lounger. They already obliterated one earlier, and were given a bit of a lecture from a member of staff but it doesn't seem to have stopped them trying again.

How did I end up in this situation? I wonder angrily.

"This holiday is going to be amazing!" Kate had insisted two days ago as we sat on the plane to Kefalonia. "We'll call it 'Sienna's Big Single Celebration'".

"I'd really rather we didn't," I muttered, wishing my best friend would keep her voice down. "It's not exactly something I'm wanting to celebrate."

Walking in on my boyfriend of two years in flagrante with one of his female colleagues just three weeks ago was still, understandably, a bit of a pain point for me. It's bad enough to find out someone has been cheating on you: to have the visual makes it even worse. (It's pretty much imprinted inside my eyelids and the image has appeared pretty much every time I close my eyes. Sleeping has not been easy.)

Then to discover that he'd actually been shagging her on the side for nearly half of our so-called relationship - a relationship, I might add, that I had thought was about to progress to cohabitation - just really was the kick in the heart I really didn't need. Especially when he then broke up with me to shack up with her.

I suppose I should be glad we weren't actually living together by the time I discovered the truth - it would have been far more difficult to untangle our lives if that had been the case. I really wished now though that Greg hadn't given me a key to his flat. It had given me both hope for a future with him, and then ripped that future away from me when I witnessed his betrayal.

I was obviously a bit of a wreck immediately after the whole incident, and Kate decided the best way to help me move on was for us to book a holiday.

I wasn't really up for it.

I wasn't really up for doing anything, to be honest. I really just wanted to slob around in my flat, living off a diet of Haribo, and rhubarb gin, accompanied by a soundtrack of my own crying and "Modern Family" episodes. This was my life now. I went to work during the day, painted on a brave face and pretended to be a professional. Then came home and wallowed in misery, booze, and jelly sweets.

Kate would not let it go though, and that's why I found myself sitting on a plane with a plastic tumbler of over-priced lukewarm white wine in one hand, and a tiny equally overpriced tub of sour cream and onion Pringles in the other - the ultimate flying cliché - as she excitedly told me the plans she had for us.

"We'll go out for dinner every night," she said excitedly. "I've been looking up some of the restaurants on TripAdvisor, there's so many places with baked feta on the menu, you'll be in heaven!"

I do like my cheese. I felt the teeniest bit of hope unfurl inside me at the thought of baked Greek cheese, and realised the tiniest of smiles was creeping onto my lips. At the moment, I grabbed and held on tight to happiness from any source I could. I wasn't ashamed.

"The capital of the island is just over the hill from where we're staying too so we can walk over there, maybe we can even hire a car," she continued excitedly. "Or do a boat trip?"

She pressed her tumbler against mine in a vague attempt at a "Cheers". It doesn't really have the same effect with plastic but I tried to get into the spirit and took a big swig of wine.

"It'll be such good fun," she finished, smiling contentedly. "We'll get you completely over that wanker, Greg."

I'd almost started to believe her.

We'd arrived in Lassi early enough on that first day to have a couple of drinks by the pool. I started to feel a bit more relaxed, the way you do on a sunny holiday abroad.

I even posted a photo on my Facebook, that old classic "hot dogs or legs" photo of the view from my sun-lounger, holding a bottle of Mythos in my hand. (Everyone knows you need to post one of these while everyone else you know back home is still at work so you can rub it in their faces that you're on holiday and they are not - it's an unspoken law of social media.)

After a few hours baking in the late May sunshine, we excitedly put on suitably summery dresses and some light make-up and headed to one of the nearby restaurants. We gorged on baked feta, moussaka, a ten euro litre carafe of white wine, and a wee bit of baklava. It was the most I'd eaten in ages - the only time my appetite goes is when I'm heartbroken.

When we got back to our apartment complex, the pool bar was lit up and full of people and lively music. We danced and drank some more, chatting with some of the other guests, before I excused myself to slip to bed. Our flight had been early and I was knackered. "I'll come with you," Kate offered but she was still full of beans and having fun, so I told her she should stay.

That was probably a mistake, I'm now thinking, as I continue to shoot covert angry looks at the horny couple.

Because shortly after I left the bar, Kate met Jack . . . and they've been all over each other like this for close to a day and a half now.

A happy couple is bad enough... but when one half of the happy couple is the friend you came on holiday with to try to forget men . . . It's even more of a nightmare.

Chapter 1

S ienna

Now, I don't want you to think I begrudge my best friend happiness. That's really not the case. And Kate has been through a bad time of it herself recently. She deserves to have a bit of fun, and it's sweet that she and this Jack guy are so into each other.

It's just a bit galling when this holiday was meant to be about me and I've been ignored the whole time. I didn't come here to be a third wheel. I came here to try and get over my ex and have a good time with my friend.

But for the last 24 hours or so I've been completely alone.

Last night I ended up eating a burger at the pool bar because Kate vanished first thing and didn't reappear until I was in bed. That was fun. I'm being sarcastic, obviously. I hate eating alone. Am I going to have to do that again tonight?

I get she's all wrapped in Jack but doesn't she realise that abandoning me like this isn't cool either?

I'm feeling ridiculously sorry for myself.

To be fair, she did invite me to join them at the pool this morning but I declined. Sit next to that over-the-top PDA all day? I'm not a total masochist.

I turn my laser beam eyes away from them again, since the gaze does not seem to be slicing them back onto two separate entities as intended, and I stare at the pool instead. It's empty, apart from a dark haired man currently swimming lengths.

Maybe I should have a swim? Who am I kidding, I've already been in and out of the pool six times today, trying to entertain myself in between reading my Kindle and walking up to the bar for another glass of wine.

There's also a pretty good chance I'm a bit tipsy now and shouldn't therefore be putting myself into a potential drowning situation. I flop back on my lounger and shut my eyes, groaning inwardly and wishing I was back under a blanket in my flat where it wouldn't matter that I was by myself.

I reopen my eyes just in time to watch the swimming guy hoist himself out of the pool like he thinks he's in some sort of cologne advert. Now, if I wasn't heartbroken, and was on the market for a bit of fun, I would definitely be into this dude. He pushes wet brown hair out of his eyes and although I've never really been sure what swoon means, I'm pretty sure that's what I do at the brief glimpse I get at his face before he walks over to his lounger to towel off. His body is definitely not bad either. My eyes linger briefly on the wet shorts clinging to his tight little arse before I give myself a mental slap for being a wee perv.

It's nice though, I suppose, to know I'm still capable of feeling lust, no matter how brief. I was starting to think Greg had broken me.

I slip my sunglasses on so I can watch covertly as he gathers his belongings together and leaves the pool area. Much to my surprise though, he pauses to momentarily separate my friend and Jack. They speak briefly before he nods and walks away.

Hmmm. So is Mr Pool Hotty also a third wheel? Now that I think about it, I think he also ate at the bar last night, watching the football on the TV. Deep in thought, I close my eyes again and drift off to sleep for a bit.

There's no sign of my friend when I wake up and she's not in the apartment either. I find a note there though saying "Gone out with Jack for a bite to eat!x"

Surprise sur-fucking-prise. Looks like it's going to be a bar meal for one for me again.

Muttering expletives under my breath most of the time, I shower and then dig through my suitcase (I find unpacking a chore so I generally just don't do it) for my pale pink midi dress, before quickly getting ready and walking down to the pool bar. It's still sunny so I order a wine and sit at a table beside the pool while I consider my next move.

I can't keep doing this all week, I think to myself. We're here until Wednesday morning and it's only Friday today. Four more days of being left alone is going to drive me crazy. I can feel myself welling up with angry tears and I blink them away as quickly as possible.

And that's when I spot him.

Chapter 2

S ienna

Mr Pool Hotty is sitting in a shady part of the bar, sipping a pint while he reads a book.

Without really thinking about it, I grab my drink and bag and walk towards his table. "Are you with Jack?" I ask before I've even reached him.

He doesn't look up from his book. "He's my brother."

Ah. Yeah, okay, there is a family resemblance, I suppose. Pool Hotty is far better looking in my opinion though. He's got one of those chiseled faces, all cheekbones and long straight lines, the angles softened slightly by a dimple in each cheek. Jack's face, from what I've noticed of it when it's not been stuck to Kate's, is nowhere near as defined; like someone tried to trace Hotty to create a duplicate but was maybe a wee bit under the influence of drugs at the time.

Pool Hotty has short dark hair but a lot of it and it's been styled into sort of a messy quiff at the front which I really want to just stick my hands in. Even better though, he's now wearing black-framed glasses - a good looking guy in glasses has always been a weakness of mine.

And I'm definitely at my weakest right about now.

I quickly remind myself that I'm not remotely interested in ever getting involved with a guy ever again. Even one who looks like this.

"Well, can you ask your brother to cool it with my friend? The pair of them are running my holiday," I find myself wailing plaintively.

He looks up at that, his eyes narrowing speculatively as he takes me in. I realise then that he has very green eyes - so ridiculously green in fact that I would have assumed he had coloured contacts in were he not already wearing those glasses.

"Do you think I haven't tried?" He asks finally. "My main goal for this holiday wasn't exactly to be stuck by myself all the time either."

Oh well, at least it's not just me suffering. Misery loves company and all that so I ask "Can I sit here?"

"If you must," he nods, indicating the chair opposite him and looking back at his book.

Charming. But I don't want to spend another minute alone so I huff audibly and settle myself in my new seat.

He doesn't say anything else and I wonder if me coming over here was a completely pointless exercise. I sip my wine, looking around the bar awkwardly, before my eyes almost involuntarily latch back onto his face.

He really is incredibly handsome. The fact he is completely ignoring me doesn't negate that, sadly.

"I'm used to my own company," he says finally, eyes still on his book. "I like being alone and I'm happy that way." I wonder if this is my cue to leave but then he continues. "But I came on this holiday thinking I was actually going to bond with my sibling for a change . . .and then discovered my brother had other ideas." He smiles ruefully, his dimples deepening as he raises his eyes to me, and I'm caught in that intense green gaze again. "You?"

"My friend brought me here to cheer me up as I got dumped three weeks ago," I say lightly. Try to say lightly. My voice is coming out thick somehow and betraying me. "Instead I've spent the last 36 hours alone, wishing I was home because there's less to distract me here. At least if I was alone in my own home it would be on my own terms, but I'm somehow even more in my own head here." A short sharp sob escapes my mouth and he looks mildly horrified. "Sorry, it's been an emotional few weeks." I rub my fingers under my eyes, checking for rogue mascara.

I should be mortified about having a mini-breakdown in front of Pool Hotty but I can't even bring myself to be. Is this rock bottom? Or do I still have further to fall?

"Well, I think we can agree that my brother and your pal are both being a bit selfish," he says softly.

"A bit?" I snort. "Try a lot."

He laughs. It's a welcome sound to my ears. "I'm Joe, by the way." He closes his book and holds out a hand.

"Sienna," I reply, putting my hand in his. God, it's so nice to be touched by a guy again, even just a hand-shake. I've missed that. I feel pathetic.

"Are you okay, Sienna?" Joe asks gently. He hasn't re-moved his hand. I feel teary again.

"It's just good to . . . Talk to someone," I say finally. "I've barely spoken to anyone since Wednesday night and I'm going out of my mind."

He gives my hand a comforting squeeze before he lets go. There's a sympathetic half-smile lifting his lips.

"Kate had all these plans for us here, I wasn't partic-ularly wanting to go on holiday in the first place but I thought . . . At least I'd be distracted. And now . . . I just . . ." I properly start to cry now. Fuck, this is embarrassing.

"Here." He carefully pushes a napkin into my hand. "Just let it out. You'll feel better, I promise."

"I feel like a fucking idiot," I bleat through my tears, pressing the napkin to my eyes.

"You're not." Joe pushes back his chair and stands up. "Give me a wee minute."

Oh crap, he's going to run away isn't he? If the roles were reversed, that's probably what I would do. I wipe away frantically at my tears, cursing myself inwardly for having no control over my emotions.

A moment later he places a shot glass in front of me. "I think you need something stronger than wine." There's a smile in his voice. He returns to his chair. "Hope you like sambuca."

"It's been a while since I last had it, but yes," I reply. We clink our glasses together and then throw the liquid down our throats. It burns and then floods my insides with a welcome warmth.

"So I have a proposition for you," Joe says after a few beats of silence. I look up at him curiously and he's watching me intently with those startling eyes.

"Okay . . ." I say slowly, tentatively. What if it's a sex-related proposition? I suddenly wonder out-of-nowhere, swallowing a nervous giggle. Not that I would do anything, obviously (still heartbroken, remember?). It's just that the way he's looking at me makes me . . . Feel things. Things I shouldn't really be feeling.

Instead he says the last thing I expect, but somehow was secretly hoping he would say.

"Sienna," he says softly. "Would you like to spend the rest of your holiday with me? I can be your substitute holiday buddy, if you want. "

Despite myself, I find myself smiling. "Joe, I thought you'd never ask."

Chapter 3

J oe

Somehow in space of five minutes I've went from being abandoned by my brother, to acquiring a new holiday companion.

I don't really know what made me do it. The fact Sienna was really upset and I didn't know how to fix things for her? Because I feel the tiniest bit guilty for my brother stealing her friend? Or is it simply because I think she's gorgeous?

I noticed her two afternoons ago climbing onto the airport transfer bus; even when she was clearly knackered from the early flight, she stood out.

Now, sitting in front of me, despite her bout of crying, she is still beautiful. Her eyes, which I thought at first glance were brown, are actually an unusually dark shade of blue. Which I guess makes more sense as her hair is so light it's practically platinum. Her eyebrows and lashes are much darker but it somehow works with her delicate features. She has a sprinkling of light freckles dancing along her cheeks and across her nose. In a word, she's amazing.

Is she my usual type? Well, according to a lot of folk, my type is simply "female". I've tried my best to lose that reputation over the years but some things still stick unfortunately. I may have made a concerted effort to change, but most people have long memories.

Maybe doing this good deed for Sienna will help atone further. Although it will benefit me just as much as I don't think she'll be difficult to spend time with. As Joey in Friends (I believe) once said, there's no such thing as a selfless good deed.

The fact she's heartbroken also means that, despite the fact I think she's hot, I'll keep it platonic - there's yet another test for me, I tell myself wryly.

I snap myself out of my thoughts and clap my hands together. "So we need a plan," I say. I open the blank back page of my book and grab the pen out of my shirt pocket. "Tell me what you were planning on doing, and we'll try and make as much of it happen as possible."

"Oh god," she sighs. "It was Kate who had all the ideas, I just listened." She takes another sip of her wine, thinking. "She said something about the capital of the island being over the hill, I think."

"Argostoli, that's right. I actually walked over to it yesterday." I needed to do something. "It's really nice, lots of good places to eat, great views. We can definitely make that happen."

"Yay," she says feebly. I smile at her in what I hope is a reassuring way.

"She talked about hiring a car, boat trips . . ." Sienna exhales loudly again. "I wish I'd paid more attention but I was exhausted on that flight."

"I know," I say without thinking, remembering again her face from the transfer bus, to which she gives me a strange look, and I feel myself blush. What the fuck? I don't think I've ever blushed in my life, despite the amount of embarrassing things I've done. Looking for a distraction, I spot a row of leaflets sitting on the bar and retrieve them.

"I can see about hiring a car tomorrow," I say, pushing some leaflets towards her. "See if there's anything that takes your fancy in amongst these attractions."

She shuffles through them. "Fiskardo looks nice," she comments after a few moments. "Let's get that on the list."

"Cool." I scrawl it down. "Anywhere else?"

"Ooh, Xi Beach?" She points out a photograph of a reddish beach to me. To my relief, she's starting to perk up a bit. She's starting to look less . . . defeated and more like the happy beauty I spotted at the pool bar on Wednesday night. Before my bloody idiot brother ruined her trip by falling for her friend.

We come up with a few more ideas, then I hear a strange little growling noise. She starts laughing and covers her face. "Oh my god, I'm so sorry. That was my stomach." She shakes her head. "I've not eaten anything apart from a croissant this morning, I've been too stressed."

"Fuck, and you've had quite a bit to drink," I jump to my feet, and grab her hand. "Come on."

"Where are we going?" She asks, letting me pull her up.

"I'm taking you to dinner, of course." She's not drinking any more on a virtually empty stomach on my watch. I take my holiday buddy role seriously.

That's what I'm telling myself anyway.

Chapter 4

Sienna

Since I acquired my new holiday friend, I am already feeling so much happier.

With a sort-of plan in place for how I'm going to spend the rest of the trip, it's like I have hope again. I'm going to have distractions. I'm not going to have to keep remembering the day I walked into Greg's flat over and over on a loop. I'm not going to have to think about how lonely I am, while my so-called bestie flaunts her newfound love in front of me.

And, to top it off, the person who is going to help distract me is exceedingly easy on the eye. So rather than think about my ex, I can try really hard not to end up falling for my saviour.

Which actually might be pretty difficult.

Because within the space of a couple of hours, I've learned that Joe isn't just a pretty face. He's clever. He's charming. He's funny. And, most importantly, he's kind. He's looked out for me and made sure I was okay, and I'll be forever grateful for that.

He's also somehow familiar. This feeling has crept up on me throughout the evening and I've not been able to shake it. Have we met before?

"Where do you stay?" I ask him now, forking up my last bite of lamb stifado, and sighing in delight that I'm back in a bustling restaurant after last night's lonely meal nightmare.

"Glasgow, although I only moved back a couple of years ago," he replies. "I was in London for a good few years. You're a weegie too, right?"

I nod. "Well, an honorary one anyway. Grew up a couple of miles south. Moved to the city after uni and been there ever since."

"No place quite like it." He has such a nice smile.

"I was just wondering if we'd met before somehow," I say. "There's something so familiar about you."

He freezes and it looks like a muscle in his cheek twitches as my words sink in. But he covers it with an easy shrug. "Must just have one of those faces," he says lightly.

He definitely definitely does not have one of those faces. I drop it for now though. I'm sure I'll figure it out at some point.

We both order a Metaxa, laughing when the waiter warns us we might find it strong. "Mate, we're Scottish," Joe jokes. "Have you ever tasted whisky?" The waiter nods, as if to say "fair play" and leaves us.

"We should probably make a toast," I suggest. "The start of a beautiful friendship and all that. "

"Good idea." Joe smiles again. He takes off his glasses, hooking them on his shirt pocket. Jeez, his eyes are even greener without them. They're quite mesmerising. Consider me hypnotised.

I remind myself again that I can't crush on this dude. I've sworn off all men. And it's not like Joe has given me any hint he's interested. He's way out of my league.

But holy shit is he hot.

He picks up his Metaxa and holds it up towards me. "Here's to an amazing few days in Kefalonia," he says softly. "Yamas."

"Yamas," I echo, falling into those amazing eyes as I sip. Finding myself thinking, traitorously, Greg who?

Chapter 5

Joe

When I get back to the apartment I've been sharing with Jack an hour or two later, he's not back yet. God knows where he and Kate are, I think, shaking my head. Probably shagging on the beach or something.

Incidentally, that's something I've never enjoyed. It's bloody uncomfortable. And the sand just ends up everywhere. Trust me.

I rub my eyes tiredly and figure it's probably time to turn in anyway. I need to get up early and do some car rental research. I don't know why it's so important to me but I'm determined to make sure Sienna enjoys the rest of her holiday.

Just seeing her light up tonight was enough to make me want more. It's pathetic she's ended up in this situation. But I'll do everything I can to make her smile. Within reason, obviously.

It feels like I've barely fallen asleep when a noise wakes me up. Several noises. A keycard beeping, a lock clicking, a door flying open and hitting the wall. Followed by lots of "shhhh" and giggle sounds.

You have got to be kidding me.

I'm suddenly extremely glad I forked out the extra money for a two bedroom apartment. Although from the noises still emanating directly outside my bedroom door, it appears Kate and Jack have decided to begin their foreplay in the hall.

This is not fun.

I mean, it probably is for them. But I'm the one who has to listen to it.

"Don't," I hear Jack mutter. "We'll wake up my broth- oh my god!" I hear a thud against the wall and a long moan. I can probably make an educated guess as to what Kate is doing to him right about now. I don't particularly want to think about it though.

I roll onto my side and curl the pillow around my head so I can try and smother out the noise. It's easier said than done. For someone who didn't want to wake me a couple of minutes ago, Jack is being surprisingly vocal. When he finally, presumably, orgasms, I can still hear it in surround sound, albeit slightly muffled.

"You are a fucking goddess," he informs Sienna's friend. I'm still cringing as they finally leave the hallway and his bedroom door shuts.

The relief is short lived as it's only a couple of minutes before the sex noises ramp up again, and turns out Kate is also pretty determined to make her voice heard.

I try two pillows, I try burrowing myself under the covers but it's far too warm and these walls are way too thin. I try earphones but blasting music into my ears isn't exactly going to help me sleep either.

Eventually I have to give up. I grab my pool towel, and mosquito repellent and wander down to the pool. I'll actually find it easier to sleep outside, mozzies or not, than in the next room from the mad shaggers.

Is every night going to be like this? I wonder, as I settle onto a lounger and cover myself with the towel. I'm not sure I can hack that. It reminds me of my younger days, back when I thought I could do whatever I wanted, sod other people's feelings and any other consequences. I don't really like reliving those times.

Sleep still isn't coming easy. I'm running high on irritated adrenalin now so I pull out my book and try to read that for a bit. I must finally drift off to sleep though . . . I only realise when someone lightly touches my arm and I start awake. A vision in white comes into focus, smiling worriedly at me.

It's Sienna, smiling ruefully at me.

"I thought I might find you out here," she says.

Chapter 6

S ienna

The poor guy is sleeping on his side on a sun lounger when I come down to the dimly lit pool to check if he's there. He looks so uncomfortable. His book has slipped to the ground and his glasses are askew. I feel some sort of emotion I can't quite identify clench my insides at the sight of his handsome face.

When I woke up, still alone, at three in the morning, to discover a text from Kate saying she was going to Jack's apartment, I thought it might be a good idea to check the pool area. I knew Joe had said they had separate rooms, but I also knew a couple of salient facts about Kate which made me suspect sleeping in the room next door wouldn't be too easy. I'm therefore unsurprised to find Joe here.

When I gently rouse him, his eyes flutter open and he seems confused. "Sienna, what . . .?" He mumbles, righting his glasses and rubbing his face. Holy crap, even half asleep with his hair all over the place, he's still unbelievably attractive.

"Come on," I pull him to his feet and help him collect his belongings. "You're coming to my apartment. You can bunk up with me"

We only have a studio so there's only one main room, comprising of the beds and kitchen area, plus the en suite. I'm extremely glad therefore that Kate didn't decide to bring Jack back to ours for a shagging session as there would have been less privacy, and even less space. So much so, it would have practically been a menage a trois, with me as an unwilling third participant.

"Do you want a water or juice or anything?" I ask opening the fridge after I've let us in. We stocked up on lots of water, Fanta Limon and Mythos on the first day. It's barely been touched thanks to Kate's absence.

"A water would be great, thanks," Joe replies. "I'm parched." I toss him a bottle, which he fumbles to catch. Still not quite awake. Adorable. I lean against the kitchen worktop, sipping from my own already opened bottle.

He takes a long swig from the bottle and then looks at me curiously, smiling. "How did you know?" I realise what he's asking.

"I got a message from Kate to say she was going back to your apartment. I figured it was going to be a bit noisy."

He raises an eyebrow questioningly, propping himself up against the wall across from me.

"She's been single a while," I shrug in response. "And also, I used to live with her... she can be bit of a screamer." I wince. I spent many a night trying to hide under my pillow back in the day.

"That," he says, shaking his head. "Was sadly accurate."

"So you got the full show?"

"Most of it."

"Listening to other people having sex," I say. "Isn't much fun." My voice has went husky all of a sudden.

Joe regards me steadily over the rims of his glasses. Sexy. "No." He agrees. "It's not."

Something has just shifted, and it's changed the atmosphere between us. Probably the fact we're talking about sex. Oh, and he's topless. That would do it.

There's a couple of beats of silence. Loaded silence. His mouth curves upwards and his eyes flash emerald. I can feel my cheeks redden.

My insides contract involuntarily again. This time I know exactly why.

"Anyway, you can catch some kip here," I say hurriedly, breaking the spell. "It's only fair." I indicate Kate's bed. In typical holiday apartment fashion, it's pushed close to my own bed. "I'm assuming she's probably not going to be sleeping here much now anyway."

"Thanks Sienna," he says softly. "I really appreciate it." He removes his glasses and slides under the sheet, moving about as he tries to get comfortable. At least it'll be an improvement over a lounger - they're not even comfortable to lie on when you're trying to sunbathe.

I slip into my own bed and switch off my bedside lamp. I curl up on my right side although I know I inevitably will wake up on my left side with no recollection of when I shifted.

"Sienna?" he whispers into the darkness after a minute or two.

"Yes?" I ask sleepily.

"I just want you to know . . . You're safe with me," he says. "I know I'm a virtual stranger and I appreciate you trusting me enough to share your space. But I promise I won't lay a finger on you."

His words should reassure me and I know that's his intention.

But I also get the unsaid message behind them; that despite that brief moment of heat between us there, he doesn't intend for it to go any further.

"Okay. Good to know," I say coolly. And I close my eyes tightly and try to force sleep to take away the sudden disappointment flooding through my veins.

Chapter 7

Joe

Daylight is filtering through the blinds in the apartment when I wake up from my third attempt at sleep. It takes me a minute to work out where I am, then it all comes screaming back to me, Kate-style.

I'm facing Sienna who is still sleeping soundly, her breathing even. She's obviously been too hot during the night as she's thrown the sheet off and . . .

Oh god, her silky white vest top has slipped down to reveal a small pale pink nipple. I suck in my breath. Her bed is so close to mine I could reach out and touch it right now. Tweak it. I give myself a mental shake.

Wasn't it just a few hours ago I gave that speech about what an honorable person I was and how I wouldn't touch her?

And that speech in itself was prompted by the fact that we definitely had just had what I could only describe as a moment, alone together in her room in the middle of the night, and if she had made the first move there was absolutely no way I wouldn't have went there. I don't think I could have resisted.

So I felt like I needed, somehow, to lay down a boundary.

I'm a fucking idiot.

She starts to stir and I panic, close my eyes and feign sleep. I hear a slight intake of breath - she's obviously realised the wardrobe malfunction - and I hear a rustle as she adjusts herself. She sits up. Everything feels really silent all of a sudden. I'm very aware of how quickly I'm breathing.

"You're awake, aren't you?" She says bluntly, breaking the stillness. "You saw my fucking nip-slip, didn't you?"

My face instantly gives me away at her words. "Afraid so," I reply, opening my eyes and squinting at her apologetically. "I was trying to protect your modesty."

"Aw shucks, you're all heart, aren't you?" She snipes but with good humour. She unfolds herself from the bed and walks over to the kitchen area. "You want a croissant? They're chocolate ones."

"Sure."

As she's handing one to me, the apartment door swings open. "Sienna, I need to tell you . . ." Kate bounces into the room and stops abruptly when she sees me too. "Oh," she says smugly. "It's like that, is it?" She looks the pair of us up and down, adds two and two together and comes up with five.

"No, I think you'll find that I had to rescue Joe from sleeping outside because you and Jack were making way too much noise," Sienna snaps, an angry flush spreading over her face.

"Oh." Kate's hand flies to her mouth, looking a bit embarrassed. She glances at me. "Sorry Joe," she adds. I shrug. "I didn't realise we were being so loud."

"Joe," Sienna says pointedly. "If it happens again, you can feel free to have Kate's bed again. Because it proba-bly will happen again." She marches over to the fridge and pulls out a can of Fanta, opening it while glaring confrontationally at her friend.

It's definitely time for me to leave. "Look, I'll take my croissant to go," I say, picking up my other belongings. "I need to try to sort out a car for us anyway. Will I meet you at the pool in a couple of hours, Sienna?"

Her face softens as she smiles at me, gratefully, her blue eyes sparkling. "That sounds like a plan, thanks Joe."

She's so bloody cute. I'm in such dangerous territory here.

Right now, I can't seem to care though.

Chapter 8

S ienna

Left alone with me, Kate turns to me and sighs. "I'm sorry, Sienna," she says softly. "I've been a shitty friend the last few days."

I'm not letting her off the hook that easy. I nod. "You have."

"I just - I got so caught up in Jack, I've not felt like this about anyone in so long. But I woke up this morning and I realised I'd barely saw you in two days, hadn't even bothered to check you were okay. And I know you hate being alone at the moment." She bites her lip, and looks pleadingly at me with her big brown eyes. "I'm here now though. We'll make it work somehow."

I feel myself softening. "You really like Jack, don't you?"

She flops backwards onto the bed, a goofy smile spreading across her face. "I do, I really do. I feel like it has potential to be more than just a holiday romance."

"Then don't worry about it." I shrug. "I appreciate the apology, Kate. I'm not going to lie, I've had a crappy couple of days and you've really pissed me off. But I'm going to spend the rest of the holiday with Joe, so you're off the hook."

"So what's going on there?" She asks curiously. "Are the two of you . . .?" She raises her eyebrows suggestively and smirks.

"Nope, we're just friends," I say firmly.

"He's pretty gorgeous though," she smiles. "Don't tell Jack this, but it was Joe I noticed first. Obviously, all water under the bridge now," she adds quickly. "But when I first went over to them it was Joe I had my eye on.

"He was friendly enough, but I could tell he wasn't interested in me . . . I ended up chatting to Jack and we hit it off immediately so it all worked out for the best. Jack says that Joe might as well be a monk though, he apparently just isn't bothered with relationships any-more."

Oh really? I'm curious about that. Because, despite his little speech last night, I know I've not been imagining the chemistry between me and him. I've never been the best at telling when a guy is attracted to me, but after what happened in the middle of the night, I feel sure he does.

But based on Kate's words, even if I was to give up on my self imposed guy ban to rebound firmly off Joe, he wouldn't be up for it anyway.

Which is what I've already told myself, but I'm now wondering why he doesn't do relationships, if that is indeed the case.

"What's going on inside your head?" Kate asks eagerly.

"I'm just wondering what his story is," I reply. "I don't know much about him yet. He's way too good looking to not have girls throwing themselves at him. And he actually seems like a nice guy too."

"You like him," Kate accuses, smiling.

(Yes, I admit, only to myself though. I have a bit of a crush. But I'm keeping the reins tight on it, I'm not letting it get out of control.)

"All Jack said, and he was very vague, was that Joe had a bit of a bad history with relationships so he doesn't really get involved anymore."

Curiouser and curiouser.

It's fine though. I'm not looking to get involved and if we keep it strictly platonic it means no awkwardness.

We both get ready and head down to the pool. Thankfully there are loads of free loungers and very few dickheads who have decided to lay out their towels in a prime position with no intention of using them until later on in the day. That drives me up the wall. So I'm glad that's been one less thing to worry about on this particular holiday.

"Where are you and Joe meant to be going today?" Kate asks me as we bask in the mid-morning sunshine. Jack hasn't appeared yet but Kate doesn't seem to be expecting him for a while. Maybe he's still trying to recover from their shaggathon last night.

"Fiskardo, I think." It's a picturesque fishing village to the north of the island. "Depends if he's able to get a car hired successfully, obviously."

"Yeah, it's probably a bit far to walk," she sniggers.

I swat her lazily with my nearest hand and, and close my eyes. I'm actually knackered due to my unsettled sleep . . . Weirdly enough though once Joe was there with me I slept far better. Maybe I felt safer?

About an hour later I feel a light touch on my shoulder. It's the briefest of contact, a light swipe of one finger down my arm to get my attention, but I feel like all the nerve endings on my skin are vibrating. I open my eyes to see Joe perching on the neighbouring lounger, grinning at me.

What is he doing to me?

I've never really believed in lust at first sight. But Joe is quickly causing me to lose faith in my entire belief system.

His green eyes are twinkling. "I've got a car," he tells me. "Do you want to go to Fiskardo now?"

I'm pretty sure I'd go anywhere with him.

Chapter 9

Joe

I'm on holiday, the sun is shining, and I've got a beautiful girl in the car beside me. What more could I need?

Just need to get the hang of driving on the wrong side of the car on the wrong side of the road. It goes against all my instincts but I'm sure I'll get used to it again in no time - it's just a rite of passage when renting a car abroad really.

"Do you drive?" I ask Sienna.

She shakes her head. "I can but I don't. I mean, I passed my test but I've never actually had a car and I never really liked driving so I've barely driven since." She smiles. "I could probably do it in an emergency but even then I would be reluctant."

"Remind me not to get into any accidents around you," I reply, only half-joking.

"I know, I'm a regular Mother Teresa," she deadpans. "Speaking of not getting into accidents, I'm assuming you're safe to drive without those, or are you already risking both our lives?" Reaching over, she lightly flicks the glasses in my shirt pocket.

"You're in good hands, I only need them to see close up." I say.

"Just thought I'd better check," she laughs, leaning forward and fiddling with the radio. It's tuned into what is presumably a local Greek station. "How old are you?" She asks suddenly.

"Ah, so you now think I must be ancient cos I need glasses to read?" I tease. "What age do you think I am?"

"I have literally no idea," she replies. "I am absolutely useless at telling ages. I'd be the shittest bouncer ever; no one would actually get in to the club because I would have to ID every single person in the queue. If I guessed, I'd probably just end up insulting you. Oh, wait, I know!" She exclaims, clapping her hands together. "What's your birthday number one?"

"My what?"

"What was number one in the Top 40 the week you were born?" She explains patiently. "If you tell me that then I can guess how old you are. It's a unique talent of mine."

I glance at her skeptically. "Really?"

She nods. "Yep." Then she wrinkles her nose and sniggers. "Well, I can guess but I didn't say I'd necessarily get it right."

I can't help but laugh. Now she's let her guard down a bit, Sienna is really funny. "I tell you what, I'll look it up later and then you can guess, okay? So what's your birthday number one then?"

"Joe, you know you're not meant to ask a lady her age, right?" She sticks her tongue out at me then relents. "Do you remember that La Bamba song? That's mine." She hums it quietly but enough for me to vaguely recall it.

"Ah yeah..." I'm pretty sure that was out in the late eighties which must put her at a similar age to me. I take a mental note to look that up later too.

"Forget horoscopes, you can tell a lot about a person from their birthday number one," she says darkly. "I went out with an older guy for a bit who turned out to be a bit of an arsehole and his song was 'Don't Stand So Close to Me' by the Police. And, trust me, by the end of that relationship I didn't want him anywhere bloody near me. Anyway, enough about my terrible relationship history." She shudders and throws me a glance. "How about yours?"

"Sorry?" I pretend to concentrate on the road. Well, I am concentrating on the road, obviously, but I focus extra hard. Or at least try to.

"Your past relationships? I'm assuming you must have some bad stories to tell? Most of us do." She sighs. "Don't even get me started on the guy who signed himself up for a dating website a month before he broke up with me . . . And don't ask me how I know that. I'm not proud."

"I kinda want to ask," I admit.

I also very much don't want to talk about my relationship horror stories. Especially given the fact that I was probably the horror in them.

She's momentarily distracted as she tells me - with more than a hint of pride actually - how she worked out the guy's password and read all his messages, and I look for my opportunity to change the subject completely.

I realise I actually do want to tell her the truth, despite the fact we barely know each other. But then she's looking at me right now as if she likes me and respects me and thinks I'm a decent guy . . . And while I like to think that is the case now - and has been for a good few years - I don't want her to start judging me based on my past, misguided actions.

She already thinks I seem familiar though, and there's a chance she might place me eventually. Would it be better just to be honest?

Or does it really matter when we've only got a few days to spend together and then we'll never see each other again anyway?

And why does that thought, already, make me feel a bit sad?

Chapter 10

S ienna

Joe clearly thinks I haven't noticed he's dodged my relationship question; he thinks he's gotten away with it.

But he hasn't. I one hundred percent knew what he was doing when he distracted me, I could tell he was stalling and was unwilling to give me any information about his love life.

Fair enough, that's his perogative not to share with a girl he barely knows. I get it.

I would like to know for sure that he's single though. Despite what Kate told me earlier, I keep thinking he's possibly in a relationship, but maybe one of those ones that would be described as "It's complicated" on Facebook. Maybe it's new, maybe it's secret. Or maybe they're "on a break".

Look, I don't want to know for my own ulterior motives. (Don't shake your head at my delusion please!) I just want to be sure there's not some girl somewhere who would be unhappy that he's currently spending his time with another girl. I've always been a girls'-girl through and through and I'd hate to be in that situation myself. And with that thought in mind . . .

"Are you single?" I ask abruptly. We're nearly at Fiskardo and we've been quiet for the past ten minutes or so. And I need to know.

"Yes," Joe replies without hesitation. He doesn't even seem surprised that I asked.

"Good." I feel myself blushing. "Sorry, just realised I would have felt really uncomfortable if you had an other half and were still helping me out like this."

"In the nicest possible way," he says, keeping his eyes straight on the road. "I wouldn't have been comfortable with that either and if I did have a girlfriend who wasn't here I wouldn't have suggested this arrangement."

"I'm glad to hear that." My voice sounds strange to my own ears.

"Like I said before though, you have nothing to worry about with me. This is strictly platonic."

His voice is gentle, and his words tactful, but he looks pissed off. The dimples are virtually nonexistent, his chiselled face hard, his lips set in a straight line.

"Of course." I clear my throat and rub my face uneasily. I've made things awkward. And forced him to remind me, once again, that he's not interested in me.

We pull up in Fiskardo in silence again, although it's less comfortable, less companionable, than it was before. I think Joe senses I'm a bit hurt as when we walk away from the car he throws an arm over my shoulder and hugs me to him briefly. It's the first proper physical contact we've had since we first met, I realise.

"Listen, I'm sorry if I came across a bit blunt there," he says softly into the side of my head. "I was concentrating on the road and I'm a guy - you know what we're like at multi-tasking." His warm breath tickles my ear and, despite the temperature being in the mid-twenties, I struggle not to shiver.

I also force myself not to point out that he was multi-tasking fine when the conversation wasn't quite as loaded. But I resolve to myself to keep it light from now on.

"Don't worry about it," I say breezily, glancing up into those dark-lashed green eyes and trying for a carefree smile. I'm not sure it quite makes the grade, but it's a relatively decent effort, perhaps worthy of a C+.

I extricate myself from his arm and step away. I've known the guy less than 24 hours, I don't know anything about him, I remind myself furiously. And he seems kinda reluctant to tell me too much.

"How about we have a drink first, then have a wander?" He suggests. A drink sounds like heaven right now. Maybe I'll even have two. He's the one driving after all.

We find a restaurant next to the harbour and order drinks. I thought he might get a beer but he sticks to a Coke. I of course opt for a wine. We're back to relatively relaxed silence again, even though we've both discovered neither of us have any Internet signal on our phones. But we're happy to people-watch. It's not even quite midday yet (don't judge my wine, I'm on holiday, okay?) but the small harbour area is already bustling with tourists.

"It's nice here," Joe says finally. "I've read reviews that say it's a bit overrated, but I'm glad we came."

"Me too." I nod. I watch people pass us - in groups, in pairs, alone - hearing snippets of different languages in short bursts. "Do you ever think about all the people in the world that you'll never meet?" I ask, almost thinking out loud. "Like, all these people walking by, they all have their own lives, and we know nothing about their stories, and probably never will?"

Joe doesn't reply and when I look around at him, I am surprised to see him watching me with a crooked smile on his face, his eyes soft and crinkling around the edges."Do you literally just say whatever is on your mind all the time?" He asks quietly, a hint of laughter in his voice.

"I've been told on more than one occasion that I have no filter," I admit, blushing at his close scrutiny.

What I don't confess, however, is the fact that I'm only like this with a select group of people. Usually people who have known me a long time, like Kate, or my family, perhaps a few of my more likeable colleagues.

I'm not sure why or how Joe has already managed to slot himself into this category. Usually I'd be more likely to clam up around a handsome bloke than turn off my filter.

So maybe it's for the best that he's not interested in me. Because God only knows what my next unfiltered monologue will be about.

Chapter 11

J oe

Sienna definitely intrigues me.

Sometimes I think she's rooting about inside my head because she almost voiced exactly what I was just thinking about.

Of course, my thoughts had headed off in a slightly different tangent. I too had been thinking how many people in the world I'd never meet . . . But then considering for the first time how weird it is that fate completely determines who of those strangers you do meet.

Okay, you can make the decision to walk up to someone in a bar and start talking to them. But what made you end up in that bar? In that town, in that country? What caused that other person to be there too?

And so, my mind had drifted and I thought of all the factors that could have been prevented me from sitting here, now, opposite Sienna.

If she hadn't been dumped, for example. Or if I hadn't suggested to my brother we go on holiday, in an apparently misguided attempt to bond with him.

If we hadn't chosen the same flight, resort, apartment complex.

If Jack and Kate hadn't decided to hook up and abandoned us both.

Or even if Sienna hadn't decided to approach me at the bar yesterday.

Where would I be right now? There's a chance I could have hired a car anyway and be sitting here in Fiskardo, but Sienna wouldn't be with me. Maybe she'd still be stewing alone. Maybe Kate would be with her. Or maybe she'd have found someone else to be her holiday buddy?

I mean, I know the film "Sliding Doors" isn't exactly dripping in Academy Awards but it makes a thought-provoking point, doesn't it? (And to be fair, it's actually not a bad film. There. I said it.)

When you ask most couples or even friends how they met, it's all ultimately down to chance. Timelines matching up somehow. It's scary how many strangers could have been in your life and become something more but due to a shift in fate they never will.

And sometimes, like in this case, everything is right apart from the unfortunate timing of it all.

Anyway, I was getting all profound, thinking this as we sat there, Sienna had spoken. Actually out loud, un-like me. My thoughts are far too muddled to enunciate clearly. Which is a bit ironic given that my fucking liveli-hood depends on me being able to do just that.

I stand and throw money down on top of the bill. "Shall we go?" I ask briskly. I could do with a proper drink, to be honest, but I really need to keep my wits about me for driving these unfamiliar roads. I'll make up for that later.

She hurries after me. "That reminds me, I owe you money," she says breathlessly. "You paid for dinner last night and for the car too."

"Don't worry about it." The one issue I definitely don't have is money.

"Okay, then I'll pay dinner tonight then," she insists. Fine. I nod, accepting her offer.

We briefly wander around Fiskardo before we head back to the car. It's definitely a beautiful little village. "I'd love to return," Sienna says dreamily. "Stay in one of those buildings overlooking the beach with the loungers next to the sea." I can almost feel her longing for it, and

I'm shocked at myself that I'm wishing to return and stay there too. With her.

I suspect I'm in big trouble.

"Where now?" She asks, breaking into my thoughts again.

"You'll see."

About 40 minutes later I'm directing the car down a steep, twisting, winding road and Sienna is gasping at the beach in front of us. "Oh my god, it's amazing!" She cries. Myrtos Beach is covered in small white pebbles and the waves rolling in seem to be bright blue. As soon as I park, she grabs her beach bag and runs out of the car without a word. I think she might have forgotten I'm here.

I'm reaching for my own beach stuff when I remember Sienna's question about my birthday number one. I squint quickly at my phone and I actually seem to have a signal so I slip my glasses on and load up Wikipedia. It doesn't take me long to find the song that was number one the week I was born.

"For fucks sake," I mutter to myself. How fucking fitting. I toss my glasses on the dashboard and follow Sienna onto the beach.

She's already laid out her towel and secured the sides of it down with her bottle of suncream, her Kindle, her sunglasses and one sandal in each corner to stop it flying away. She's now in the process of removing her other sandal and wriggling out of her dress. I'm trying hard not to watch as I start spreading my own towel now but I can't help myself.

Obviously I've already witnessed her in a bikini at the pool; but it means I already know she has a banging body and it makes me want to look even more at how hot she is in that bright pink bikini. She catches me, and I'm surprised to see her lips curl into a pleased smile as she glances quickly away again. It seems she likes me looking at her.

She walks towards the water and I hastily remove my shirt so I can follow. I want to stay close to her.

The more time I spend with Sienna, the more my resolve weakens. I keep telling her it's strictly platonic but I really don't want it to be.

And I'm pretty sure she feels it too.

Chapter 12

S ienna

A few hours later, I'm back in my apartment and showering before dinner. And I'm also dwelling very much on the fact that Joe and I had another moment on Myrtos Beach, while we were playing about in the sea.

We were having a bit of a playfight, splashing each other and it got a bit . . . Touchy-feely, shall we say. He'd managed to grab both my hands to stop me cupping more seawater to throw at him and we were a bit too close together, and suddenly that easy smile of his slid right off his lips and we were just staring into each other's eyes like there was no one else in the world.

God, I have never had a moment like that in my life. It was like something out of a movie. I genuinely thought we were going to kiss. I could hardly even breathe in those few seconds. What a walking, talking, bare-ly-breathing cliché I am.

Then a kid on the beach screamed and the spell was broken. Joe laughed, let go of my hands, and ducked under the water completely for a few seconds, while I walked back to my towel. Glaring at the snivelling little bastard who had ruined the moment.

We didn't talk about what nearly happened, even when we were both dry again and back in the car. But it wasn't awkward or anything. Far from it. We swung between companionable silence and chatting away like old friends. Which is still weird to me when in actuality we've only been acquainted for 24 hours and I've never been good at small talk with virtual strangers. And, ac-tually, I still don't really know that much about him.

I realise, however, that we have spent most of those 24 hours together and have effectively already gone on several dates, platonic or otherwise. We're definitely past that all-important third date, that's for sure.

I roughly blow-dry my chin-length bob, slip on a lemon coloured sundress, and carefully do my make-up. Am I trying to impress him? Abso-fucking-lutely. I want him to eat his heart out. Rue the exact moment he decided not to just smash his lips onto mine. I paint my lips bright red, apparently just to emphasise my point.

It makes me angry with myself how much I already fancy the guy. Although I definitely haven't thought about Greg for nearly a full day, so every cloud and all that.

When I head down to the bar, he's already there, chatting away to the barman/receptionist, Andreas. Joe seems to be able to charm everyone when he puts his mind to it.

I stop for a moment to admire him, before he spots me. It's a bit cooler tonight than it has been and he's wearing faded jeans and a white shirt with the sleeves pushed up, revealing toned forearms. Those are very good forearms. He clearly hasn't shaved for a couple of days and the scruff running along his sharp jawline definitely works for him. He's also obviously one of the lucky folk who tan virtually within seconds of being exposed to sunshine. I find myself staring down at my much paler skin with disappointment. I am tanned but nowhere near as golden as Joe.

He glances up at me then and his eyes narrow slightly as he takes me in from head to toe. It's weird, I felt less naked when he looked at me in my bikini earlier. That look was admiring, but this one is . . . Something else entirely. His gaze is burning into me, through my clothes. His eyes . . .

Well, there's no disguising the lust in them. He is practically smouldering. For all his chat, I'm still provoking a physical reaction in him, and this makes me strangely satisfied. Even if he doesn't intend to touch me, I get comfort from knowing that he clearly wants to.

And with that thought, the naughtier side of my personality comes out to play, and I can feel my red lips curving up into a smile. I'm going to have some fun with this.

I blame the lipstick.

By the time I've walked over to him, he's composed himself. "Nice dress " He manages a smile, his voice husky. "Want a drink?"

"I'll have a gin and tonic," I tell Andreas. I slip onto the barstool beside Joe, leaning close and taking a deep inhale. "You smell so good," I tell him. He really does. I make sure I'm still close when I speak so that my breath catches his flesh.

He's flustered; I can tell by the way his own breath hitches. I feel myself smirking as Andreas passes me my drink. I pop a straw into it. "I feel much better after having a shower," I sigh, lifting my glass up and sucking up a significant amount of refreshing liquid through the straw. "I felt like I'd got sand everywhere, you know? It took so long to wash it all off my body."

He swallows. I'm pretty sure he's now thinking about me in the shower, which was absolutely my intention of course. "Yeah, I know what you mean," he manages. Quite the wordsmith, is our Joe. "I was the same."

Damn, now I'm imagining him in the shower.

Shake it off, Sienna.

I smile, and suck sharply on my straw again. He's staring at my lips, realises what he is doing, and quickly averts his gaze. Wow, I thought he'd be smoother than this. "How about a game of pool before we head to dinner?" I suggest, sliding down from the stool, drink in hand.

"Sure." Joe follows me to the table and watches me set up the balls. He pulls a coin out of his pocket. "Heads or tails?" He asks me.

"Tails," I say confidently.

I edge closer to him as he tosses the coin in the air. When he reveals the outcome on his hand, I lean forward and lightly grip his wrist as if I'm pretending to view it closely. "It's tails." I state the obvious, tapping the coin, then gently running my finger along his hand as I pull away. His eyes widen at my touch.

"Looks like it's my break then," I smile, walking away to the other end of the table. Almost unconsciously, I've added a bit of extra sway to my hips as I walk. I hope he appreciates it as it's one hundred percent for his benefit.

I line up my shot, completely aware of him watching me. "Ready for me to whip your arse?" I ask, unable to resist winking at him.

"You wish," he jokes, but that heat is back in his eyes again. Gotcha, I think to myself.

And then I send the cue ball flying into the other balls. Let's play.

Chapter 13

Joe

I'm not entirely sure what Sienna's playing at - apart from pool, obviously - but she has definitely upped the stakes tonight. And I'm losing against her. Both at pool, and at whatever this other game is.

I thought I was attracted to the cute, funny babbler who just says whatever the fuck is on her mind, cries at the drop of a hat, and looks fantastic in a bikini. But this has nothing on the goddess that has turned up tonight and appears to be doing her best to push every single one of my buttons. The fact that both of these personalities co-exist in the same petite blonde package is blowing me away.

She has potted all of her balls now and is onto the black. I'm normally decent at pool but I cannot concentrate at all on this game. I can't think why . . .

She's chalking up her cue but she's paying no attention to what she's doing. Instead she's staring directly at me, her gaze bold and unapologetic. She licks her lips, slowly and deliberately. That red lipstick is killing me.

"Prepared to lose?" she taunts. I can only shrug helplessly as she leans forward and sinks the black apparently as effortlessly as she's destroyed all my defences.

I want her so badly I'm shaking.

She walks towards me, hand extended. "Good game," she says coolly. "For me, that is." Her small hand slips into mine to shake it, her eyes challenging me. Good god, I almost lean in at that point, for the second time today almost kiss her.

But she pulls her hand away, picks up her drink and polishes it off. When she turns back around it's like her seductress personality never existed. "Dinner time?" She asks, raising her eyebrows at me questioningly. "I'm absolutely starving."

So am I, I think. But not for food anymore.

The babbler has returned with a vengeance as we walk down towards the strip. "What do you feel like eating?" she asks. "Something traditional or something else? I think I saw a pizza place, and there's a diner too. Although I really could go some more baked feta."

"What is it with you and baked feta?" I ask curiously, laughing. In the 24 hours we've been acquainted, baked feta has been mentioned at least 5 or 6 times.

She smiles, slightly embarrassed. "I just really like cheese."

She's just so fucking sweet. It doesn't matter whether she's talking about dairy products or trying deliberately to turn me on . . . Actually, she doesn't need to even try now, I'm too far gone. I turn away from her, swallowing a groan of frustration, and drag my hand down my face.

I need to cool down; I could seriously do with a cold shower right about now. And I had one already, less than an hour ago, trying to rid myself of the memory of that near-miss kiss in the sea earlier.

I hadn't known whether to be relieved or exasperated when that kid had screamed. I'd opted for a mixture of both emotions, telling myself it was for the best on one hand, while having to remain in the sea for a bit until I had - how should I put it? - visibly calmed down.

By the time I got back to my towel, Sienna was acting like nothing had happened, and I'm pretty sure she started talking about baked feta again, so there didn't feel any point in trying to broach the subject.

And how many times can I bring out that fucking platonic speech anyway? Especially when I keep contradicting it with my own actions.

In the short space of 24 hours this girl has wrecked me.

Although to be fair, if I'm being really honest, for me this has been building since I first saw Sienna on that airport transfer bus. Long before I even knew the slightest thing about her.

I remember the looks I'd covertly shot her at the bar later that same night; the feeling of intense disappointment when she left without even a glance towards me when I felt such a magnetic pull towards her.

Noticing her in the bar alone the following night, and then again last night.

I had been fully, painfully, aware of her presence on all of those occasions, but I hadn't approached her because I think, deep down, I knew she was going to test me to my limits.

And that's probably why, when she approached me, I had no choice but to offer to keep her company because I had been already thinking about her, wanting her, since the first moment I saw her.

I'm so tired of fighting my attraction to her.

"You okay?" Sienna asks. I drag myself back to the present and realise I've not yet responded to her cheese comment.

"Um, yeah. Just thinking how hard you're making it to resist trying baked feta for myself." I joke.

But, obviously, that's not all I'm finding difficult to re-sist.

Chapter 14

Sienna

Readers, it's safe to say I shat it.

That red lipstick has a lot to answer for. I became a different person while playing that pool game. I was fucking shameless. I made it perfectly clear, beyond a shadow of a doubt, that I was more than a little into Joe.

And, even better, I had absolutely no doubt that the feeling was mutual. In those few minutes, I knew he would probably do whatever I wanted, no questions asked. I was winning the game.

I held all the cards. I had all the power.

But as I shook Joe's hand, stared intently into those bright green eyes again, I realised I had no idea what the rules of the game were. I had no idea what to do next.

I simply had no game. And I got scared.

What did I even want to happen here? Yesterday morning I was still mourning my past relationship and today I was already moving on? Did I really want a holiday fling? Would that just make things even harder for me?

Half of me was fantasising about the idea of Joe just throwing me, caveman style, on that pool table and having his wicked way with me, while the other half was already realising how hard it could be to get over him if that did happen.

Maybe the moments of anticipation are better than the follow-through. Maybe I need to protect myself and see this as just a flirtation and nothing more.

And, yes, maybe I need to stop overthinking every bloody thing.

I laugh inwardly at the very idea of the flirtation turning into anything long-term as I glance across the table at Joe. Glasses now back in place, he's studying the menu and I can't help but marvel at his hotness once again. This is not a guy I can picture wanting to chill out and binge watch my sitcoms with me on my lumpy sofa. He belongs on red carpets, at nightclub openings, film premieres, after-parties.

He must feel my eyes on him because he glances up at me. "What?" He asks, raising an eyebrow. Surely he must know how sexy that eyebrow quirk is?

"I was just wondering if you watch TV," I blurt out honestly. Then want to smack myself in the head.

He laughs, puzzled. "Why wouldn't I?"

I shrug, knowing I'm blushing. He has no idea what's going on inside my brain right now. "What shows do you watch?" I quickly follow-up.

It's his turn to shrug. "Lots of stuff. Mostly comedy." Right answer. And it's provided me with a nice, easy topic of conversation that doesn't involve me trying to badly seduce him again.

The waitress appears then so after we have ordered we start to talk about our favourite sitcoms. It turns out he also likes my beloved Modern Family, and we also have shared love of The Office (both the American and British versions), Brooklyn 99 and Parks & Rec. He convinces me to try The Book Group, and Spaced, while I urge him to give Schitt's Creek a second chance. We both vehemently agree that Everyone Loves Raymond is a turd, with King of Queens coming a close second for the boobie prize.

Over starters and white wine, we discuss favourite Friends episodes - his is the one with Ross' leather trousers and mine is the one with Ross' fake tan. We agree, once again vehemently, that Ross is the best character.

"He makes a lot of silly mistakes," Joe says at one point. He grimaces, pushing his glasses up. "I can identify." Then he changes the subject before I can query this any further. "You were right about the baked feta - it was amazing."

"See, don't knock it 'til you've tried it. Always good to try new things," I say lightly.

His eyes flicker up, holding my gaze, and I feel my breath catch in my throat. "I'm definitely out of my comfort zone," he says softly. His eyes are suddenly burning into mine before he glances away, almost shyly.

My insides are humming with lust. I know he's not talking about cheese anymore.

That loaded silence looms up again; only a few seconds but it feels like minutes.

He sighs, pulling off his glasses. "I'm not imagining this, am I?" He asks quietly, deliberately not looking at me. "There's something here, between us. It's not just me, right?"

I inhale sharply. "No. It's not just you," I manage finally. Those green eyes latch back onto my face and, once again, I see the heat in them. I feel a shiver of desire run through me.

The moment is interrupted by the waitress bringing us our main courses. "Can I get you anything else?" She asks, her eyes lingering flirtatiously on Joe. She's pretty. I want to punch her.

He shakes his head. "No," he says tersely. "Thanks." She nods, clearly disappointed, and leaves us alone again.

"So this looks great," I say brightly, looking down at my plate. Wondering where my appetite has gone. I start cutting up my meat, pop a bit of potato in my mouth. Try to ignore the fact that Joe is still watching me. I can feel the frustration emanating off him.

"Sienna . . ." His voice sounds pained.

"We should probably talk about this later," I interject, looking back up at him. "In private." Despite the fact that our voices are low, I've noticed that the couple at the next table were half-listening to our Friends-related conversation, and I don't think it's the best idea to have a conversation about our mutual attraction while they're still sitting there.

"Okay." He nods, apologetically, flicking a glance at the couple. So he clearly has his suspicions too.

"In the meantime though," I say. "Maybe you could tell me a bit more about yourself. Because I feel like you've not really given me anything so far."

He hesitates. "Alright," he says eventually. "I'll tell you anything you want to know."

I smile. "Good."

Time to get to the bottom of who Joe - oh, for heaven's sake, I don't even know his bloody surname! - really is...

Chapter 15

J oe

God, I'm shitting a brick here. I have no idea what she's going to ask and that terrifies me. But if I want anything to happen here, I'm going to have to go along with this.

And I do want something to happen.

"Okay, first up: what's your surname?" She asks.

That's easy; I can do this one. I don't think she'll recognise me immediately from that. "Quinn."

She nods. "Cool. Mine is Norton." She makes a self-mocking face. "Maybe I'm a bit old fashioned but usually I like to know a guy's full name before I even consider heading off in cars with them. I really should have checked that sooner in case you were a serial killer or something."

"Fair enough."

"What do you do for a living?" is her next question.

Once again, easy enough to answer but it could raise her suspicions. "I'm a freelance journalist." I want to gloss over this one though. I add hurriedly. "You?"

She waves a hand dismissively. "I work in HR. Pretty dull. I'm definitely work to live, I don't live to work." Her eyes light up suddenly, as if something has struck her. I'll welcome anything that changes the subject. "Have you looked up your birthday number one yet?"

I nod. "It's 'Respectable' by Mel and Kim," I tell her reluctantly.

She, of course, immediately starts singing the cho-rus - "we are never going to be respectable" - while I cringe again at the song choice that according to Sienna Norton, self-proclaimed birthday number one special-ist, could say a lot about me.

She of course doesn't realise the irony of it, given she knows fuck all about my past. She's now looking thoughtful, I guess doing calculations in her head. "'87, right?"

I grin. "I'm not that old," I joke.

"Nineteen eighty seven." She narrows her eyes at me. "Yes?"

"You got me," I reply, holding up my hands.

"We're the same age then, give or take," she smiles. "I'm 34, I think you'll already be 35?"

"You're good," I admit.

"Yep, when I actually get it right I'm quite impressed with myself," she laughs. She pushes her chair back. "And now I've impressed you, I need to pop to the loo." She winks at me and wanders off in search of the bathroom.

The couple at the next table are getting ready to make a move. The guy hesitates as he passes the table and then stops completely.

"Sorry, man, this is so not cool of me, but I just wanted to say I'm a massive fan," he says. "Your book has always been one of my favourites."

I look blankly at him. It's been a long time since I've been recognised. But he seems convinced he knows who I am.

I give in. "Thanks, that means a lot," I say. And it does.

So here's my big secret. Well, a part of it . . .

Once upon a time, so long ago now that it feels like it must have been another lifetime, I wrote a book. Which got published. And sold a lot of copies.

At the tender age of 21, I was a bestselling author. And I also found myself with the 15 minutes of fame that went along with it. In fact, I probably got way more than 15 minutes and I don't think I deserved that at all.

Don't get me wrong, it's always nice hearing praise for the book. It was something I put a lot of work into, something I channelled my loneliness into when I felt like I had nothing else. It's just the other stuff, that ended up going hand-in-hand with it all, that I wish I could forget.

Because I definitely let that temporary fame go to my head for a while, started to believe my own hype. Made a few mistakes along the way.

Some of which were in the public eye.

I wince at the memory.

"So, I have to ask, did you ever see any of those girls again after . . . ?" My new pal asks me, as if reading my mind, viewing my own memories.

I don't want to have to remember this shit again. But I smile ruefully and shake my head, cutting off the end of his question as politely as I can.

"Nope, never again. Which I completely deserved."

"Shame," he says. "That Leesa girl was hot." He holds out a hand. "Anyway, it was good to meet you."

He leaves and I look up to see Sienna walking back towards the table, looking puzzled. "What was that all about?" She asks. "Was he apologising for them eaves-dropping?"

I laugh, but it's forced. "Something like that," I say lightly.

She lowers herself into her chair. Suspicion flickers in her eyes but she can't prove anything so it doesn't have anywhere to go. She picks up her fork again. "So whereabouts in Glasgow do you live?" She continues her questioning.

"Southside. Shawlands, actually."

"What a weird coincidence, me too." It turns out we only live three streets apart. "Your bit is a lot fancier than mine though," she comments. "You either must have won the lottery or be really good at your job."

"Well, I definitely didn't win the lottery," I shrug.

Sienna watches me speculatively again, obviously trying to decide what she wants to ask next. Every time it makes me nervous.

"What were you like when you were younger?" She asks finally. "At school?"

"What do you think I would have been like?" I can't help but ask in return. Somehow eager to see if her expectation meets reality. I'm fairly sure it won't.

She laughs. "I find it hard to imagine folk I've met only as adults as kids, don't you?" She takes a sip of wine. "I can only imagine you being like the way you are now, only 20 years younger. Probably cute though, rather than handsome. Maybe you hadn't quite grown into your looks yet. But confident. Friendly. Popular." She smiles bashfully. "I feel like I probably would have had a massive crush on you."

I can't help but snort at her many assumptions, although her last comment warms me. "I wasn't popular, and I certainly wasn't friendly," I reply. I try to keep the edge of bitterness out of my voice, attempt to keep my voice light. "I was definitely a nerd, although I didn't have the glasses back then. I was arrogant. And I was angry all the time."

She actually giggles at that, and the sound of it actually soothes me slightly. I don't think she meant to though, and she makes an apologetic face immediately. "Suddenly, teen you has just became even more attractive. I was always partial to a weirdo... I probably wouldn't have admitted that crush to my friends though." She hesitates. "Why were you so angry though?"

I shrug, looking away. "My parents were never happy. They took it out on us a lot, me and Jack, I think they'd thought having kids would make them complete somehow. Then it didn't and that was our fault too. Jack was always more popular than me, I don't think it bothered him as much because he just distracted himself with his friends. I was more sensitive and took it more personally. It's . . ." I bite my lip, take a deep breath before I continue "It's not nice feeling like your parents didn't really want you."

Her eyes soften and well up. She reaches over and puts a warm hand on top of mine. "That really sucks,

Joe," she whispers. "I'm sorry they made you feel that way."

I've never told anyone this before. Not someone who wasn't a mental health professional, anyway. Me and Jack don't even talk about it- not that we're particularly close. I don't know why I've chosen to open up to Sienna.

I think she senses I'm done with baring my soul for now though. "Let me get the bill," she says. "I did promise to pay for once, after all."

After she's paid, we stand up and walk back out onto the street. It's dark now, and fairly quiet, what with it being relatively early on in the season. We've been walking, both in silence, for a couple of minutes, before I realise something.

At some point, since leaving the restaurant, I've slid my hand into hers.

Chapter 16

Holy crap, Joe's holding my hand!

We've held hands before, mostly to tow each other other along when one of us is dawdling though. This is not, I repeat not, the same thing.

Somewhere outside the restaurant, I felt his fingers brush mine briefly before they laced with mine. I stifled a gasp. It seemed he wasn't even aware of doing it. But there it was.

I actually feel the moment he realises as his steps falter for a moment, and his grip loosens ever so slightly. I can feel him glance down, in the direction of our intertwined hands. Then he takes a deep shaky intake of breath, and his hold tightens again. I feel myself relax, realising my own breath had paused again while I waited to see what his reaction would be.

Something has irrevocably changed in our relationship this evening. What with my intentional flirting earlier, the acknowledgement that we were both feeling . . . feelings, and then him telling me things I feel sure he rarely speaks about, we're definitely more than just holiday buddies now.

The question is, what are we going to do about it?

We pass the last building on the strip before we have to turn off for the path up to the apartments. The silence between us is so heavy now, and I need to say something, I need to break it. I'm feeling dizzy with anticipation. And slightly terrified at the weight of my feelings.

"That was a nice restaurant, wasn't it? I'd definitely go back. The baked fe- . . ."

"Sienna," he interrupts me. He stops walking and I glance at him in surprise. His eyes are dark and heavy-lidded, and his handsome face completely serious. The dim light is catching his angular features and I can feel my insides liquidising with want.

"What?" I ask, breathlessly. I can't look away as Joe swings me around and pushes me up against the wall, his body inches from mine.

A slow irresistible smile spreads across his face. "Stop babbling," he whispers. And then he tilts my head up, bends down and kisses me.

And oh my god . . . That chemistry, the attraction that has been between us from virtually the very start? It's all in this kiss. He holds my face in his hands and his lips move against mine, softly at first, before the pressure gets harder and, with a groan, his tongue slides into my mouth.

My hands slip under his shirt and onto his back, which is warm and soft, and I can't help but notice he's trembling. I am too. I feel like I'm on the cusp of combustion, just from kissing him. How could I actually survive anything more than this, anything wilder?

Joe pulls back briefly and I see the desire in his eyes. "Jesus, Sienna," he moans, dragging his lips down the side of my face, kissing my neck. I pull him closer to me and I can feel him, hard, against me, showing me once and for all just how much he wants me. He takes my lips again, his hands tangling in my hair and tugging on it slightly, and it's my turn to moan. I kiss him back, as hard as I can, trying to show him how much I want him too.

"You are so fucking hot," he breathes into my mouth at one point, and I melt against him, glad he's apparently propping me up. He drops a few more quick kisses on my lips and then pulls back, leaving me bereft.

We stay entwined though, stare into each other's eyes for a long moment while still leaning against the wall.

"You're allowed to say something, you know," Joe says eventually. His voice comes out hoarse and rasping.

"You told me to quit babbling." I point out, my own voice uneven. "I don't want to ruin the moment."

He laughs huskily. "You're the cutest babbler I've ever met," he tells me, placing a kiss on the corner of my mouth. "I just needed to concentrate for a minute and you were about to start talking about cheese again." He smooths a hand through my hair, his eyes moving over my face intently. "You're so beautiful," he says quietly. "I'm sorry I broke my promise not to touch you but I couldn't help myself."

"Are you really sorry?" I ask, smirking. He grimaces and shakes his head, green eyes sparking with dark humour.

"Not really. I kept telling myself it was platonic but it's been getting harder and harder to deny how attracted I am to you." He looks down for a moment, as if deciding something, then back up into my eyes. "I actually wanted you from the first moment I saw you getting on the transfer bus," he admits, swallowing hard.

"You did?"

I'm totally taken aback. I hadn't realised he'd already been interested in me when I stormed up to him demanding he try to separate Jack and Kate. He hid it very well.

Guilt overwhelms me. "I didn't even notice you." I confess. He nods and presses a small kiss to both cheeks. Heat gathers where his mouth has touched.

"I know. That's okay. "

"If it's any consolation, I really fancied you from the first minute I noticed you getting out of the pool yesterday though," I smile, curling my fingers around one of the belt loops on his jeans, trying to pull him closer again.

"That does help soothe my ego a little." His lips quirk upwards. "Although it does make me wonder if you just want me for my body."

"Well . . ." I joke. "I did christen you Pool Hotty in my head before I knew your name."

Joe laughs. "Not gonna lie, I kinda like it."

We kiss again. This time it's gentler, softer, more tender, less hurried. When we pull apart this time, we're both smiling. He peels me off the wall. "We should probably head back."

"I'm not sure I can manage it," I say, giggling. "My legs feel wobbly."

He takes my hand again and grins at me, his eyes bright. "Mine too."

Chapter 17

Joe

I like this girl so much.

More than I've liked someone in a long time. Possibly more than I've liked anyone in forever?

She's pretty, she's sweet, she makes me laugh and now that I've kissed her, I don't want to stop.

But I'm going to have to. Stop. At some point. Because I didn't mean to get involved and, now I have, I need to make sure she knows this can't go anywhere.

We're back in the bar at the apartments, that same place I struggled to resist her earlier. Was that just a few hours ago? Did we really only meet yesterday evening? It feels impossible. It feels like I've known her for years.

Sienna places a bright blue cocktail in front of me and then drops down on the seat beside me, curling her legs up underneath her. "I got us Blue Lagoons," she explains. "I thought it was an appropriate choice given the fact we seem to be surrounded by them on this island."

"It makes sense. Thanks." I glance up from my phone, where I was checking my emails, and see her watching me. She's chewing on her lip, and her eyes are darker than normal. She looks like she wants to say something. "What is it?" I ask curiously.

She lets out a whoosh of air. "Just thinking how good you look in those glasses."

I laugh. I think this is now the second time she's made me blush. "These old things?" I joke, adjusting them self consciously.

She doesn't smile. "Yep. They're hot."

I've never really thought of them like that. But I like the fact that Sienna seems to enjoy them. Really seems to enjoy them, judging by the lustful expression on her gorgeous face.

She's edged closer now and she leans in to kiss me again. "Really. Fucking. Hot." she murmurs breathlessly between kisses, almost repeating my own words from earlier. As is apparently now the case when it comes to Sienna, I can't resist, and the kiss deepens.

"What's going on here then?" We pull apart to see Kate and Jack standing in front of us. Jack looks amused, Kate looks smug. I groan.

"So much for just being friends," Kate laughs. "What's changed since this morning?" She asks Sienna. A bit inappropriately, in my opinion but each to their own and all that.

Sienna shrugs, smiling at me. "I couldn't keep pretending I didn't fancy him," she says simply. Her admission makes me feel . . . weird. In a good way.

I smile back. "Likewise."

"Wow." Jack shakes his head. "Who would've thought it, the monk has feelings after all?"

I know my brother doesn't mean it in a bad way, but his words still sting. It seems he and Kate are, indeed, perfect for each other. Both geniuses at making other people feel uncomfortable.

"You want to join us for a drink?" Sienna offers. I can tell it's half-hearted and maybe they can too. Or maybe they're still too wrapped up in each other as they decline the offer.

"I think we're going to head to bed," Kate says, looking meaningfully at Sienna. "In Jack's apartment. You know, just in case you're wondering where I'll be."

"Kate, you're about as subtle as a sledgehammer," Sienna sighs. "Have a nice night."

"You too." Kate throws us an exaggerated wink.

"Be careful with him," Jack adds as they take their leave. "Don't want to scare him back to the monastery."

"For fucks sake," I mutter. I take my glasses off and rub my eyes.

"What does he actually mean by that?" Sienna asks quietly, watching them leave.

I shake my head. "First of all, it's worth noting that Jack knows fuck all about my life. He's taken a couple of sentences I said on the plane and made an assumption."

"And what did you say? I'm guessing it wasn't that you're actually a monk and heading back to the monastery immediately after the holiday," she says dryly, picking up her cocktail and taking a long swig at it.

"He was talking about holiday flings, and I said I had no intention of getting involved with anyone - I didn't exactly plan to meet you. He then asked me when I'd last been involved with someone and I don't think he expected the answer he got." I realise now she's going to want to know the answer to this too and I'm now too far in.

She just nods though. "Okay."

I blink. "You're not going to ask?"

"It's killing me not to," she smiles. "But I'm trying not to be super-nosy. I already interrogated you earlier, after all." There's about five seconds of silence. "No, sorry, you're going to need to tell me."

"It's been a long time since I've been in a relationship," I tell her. "I find it easier being alone."

"Define 'long time'." She picks up her cocktail again.

"Not since my early twenties," I say briefly. Her mouth drops open. "Don't get me wrong, I haven't quite been the monk Jack is making me out to be, it's just the relationship thing I don't do."

"Can I ask why?" Sienna doesn't seem judgemental or anything, just curious.

"It's a long story," I sigh. "I'd rather not get into it. Let's just say I made some mistakes when I was younger and it made me decide relationships were too hard. Or that I wasn't good at them anyway."

"I'm thinking the shit with your parents didn't help with that either," she says perceptively.

"Probably not. That definitely fucked me up. But I can't put all the blame on that. Lots of folk have messed-up backgrounds and still can be in fully functional relationships. I'm the problem. Sometimes I feel like . . . I'm maybe a bit broken somehow?"

Why do I keep telling her all this shit?

"I don't think you're broken." Her voice is soft. "Relationships are fucking hard. Trust me, as someone who has just emerged from one a wreck of her former self, no one gets that more than me."

"What happened there?" Now I have to pry further.

She sits back, scowling. "Let's start at the end where I went to his flat to surprise him - I had a key. As far as

I was aware, he was at work, and I was going to make him dinner because he'd been working so hard. Instead I found him in there shagging one of his colleagues."

"Fuck." I don't know what else to say.

"Now, at that point you'd think he'd be grovelling, on his knees, begging me for forgiveness, wouldn't you? But, no, he dumps me for her instead. Said it had been wrong for a while, he didn't think he had actually ever loved me." She's stirring the remains of her cocktail furiously, and then she looks up at me, dark blue eyes almost shooting sparks. "I can't be certain, as I was riding a pretty intense wave of humiliation at the time, but I'm pretty sure he actually said 'it's not me, it's you'."

"No!"

She starts to laugh, but there's no humour in it. "Seriously. I was the injured party in all of this, but he was just piling on more and more insults. And I was such an idiot, there were so many bloody red flags popping up throughout the relationship and I ignored them all."

She shakes her head. "In retrospect, I blame the pandemic. I met Greg just after we were allowed out to play again, and I'd just spent more than two months alone on lockdown. I was so sick of my own company, and then we had formed a bubble when everything locked back down again so I got way too attached and overlooked all the signs it was wrong." She frowns. "I'd like to think I'd have shown better judgement otherwise but hindsight's 20:20 and all that."

"He sounds like an absolute prick." I feel white hot rage on Sienna's behalf. I don't know how anyone could treat her this badly. She's the sweetest girl I've ever met, and she deserves so much more than that.

She deserves much more than me too, I realise. But, for now, I vow to myself, and for the next few days, I'm going to do my best to make sure I'm deserving of her. I slide my arm around her and pull her towards me so I can kiss her on the cheek.

I want any memories she has of me, of this short time we have together, to be fond ones.

Chapter 18

S ienna

My eyes flutter open and I realise it's morning. And an arm is looped around my waist. For once I've not shifted position during the night.

I can't help but smile as I think of last night, especially that heart-stopping kissing session on the way back to the apartments. I feel like I'm still floating on that memory a bit.

After the bar we came back to my room since Kate had oh-so-pointedly told us she'd be with Jack, and I was sure Joe wouldn't want to hear a live sex show again. Oh, and obviously I wanted Joe to be with me because . . . Well, those pesky feelings again.

But I also didn't want to rush things. Which I think Joe sensed as he didn't try to take things any further than kissing last night and eventually we drifted off to sleep in each other's arms in my single bed.

"Morning." His voice vibrates against the back of my neck, a warm growl that flows down through my veins and causes butterflies in my tummy. I can also feel his hard-on pressing into me and I already know there's no way either of us can stop where this is inevitably going.

But I'm absolutely ready for it now.

"Hey," I manage in return.

"Have we had any nipple incidents today?" He asks, amusement in his voice. "Do you need me to check for you?"

I glance down at my chest. "They're both covered," I report back.

Joe tuts. "Well, we can't have that." And with that, his fingers slide up and pull down my vest top. I bite back a gasp as he kisses the side of my neck and pulls on my nipple at the same time. "Much better," he says smugly, palming my whole breast.

I can't stop a moan escaping my lips this time. I feel him laugh against my neck and then next thing I'm flat on my back and he's looming over me. All flat stomach, and messy hair and wicked grin. His eyes have went dark again.

"Sienna," he says softly. "I'm afraid I'm going to need you to take all your clothes off." I hesitate for a moment, looking up at him in awe, thinking somehow he's became even sexier overnight. "Now," he nudges me on, an edge of command creeping into his voice.

Wordlessly, I pull my top over my head and he breathes in sharply, biting his lip as he looks at my bare breasts. "I've been thinking about these since yesterday morning. That was some sight to wake up to." He bends his head and kisses them both, and I quickly feel my arousal overriding any embarrassment.

"You seem to have forgotten to remove your other items of clothing," he says huskily, between kisses.

"You appear to be blocking my way," I argue, my breathing uneven.

"A good point." He nods, moving up to my lips and dropping a quick kiss on my mouth before he heads south, collecting my shorts and knickers on the way. And now I'm completely naked, absolutely exposed, in front of him.

He looks me up and down and licks his lips - I think an unconscious rather than deliberate gesture but it still sends lust shooting through my body. "You're gorgeous," he says simply, his eyes meeting mine, as he gently runs his hands up my thighs. Then he lowers his head between my legs and starts to taste me.

"Oh my god," I bite out, my fists clenching the bedsheets beneath me as he runs his tongue over me. He chuckles against me, which makes me feel even more sensitive, then slips a finger inside me.

He seems instinctively to know how to turn me on but prolong the pleasure so I don't immediately climax. I have a feeling he could make me orgasm far quicker if he really wanted to. He's clearly in no hurry though. And because of this I feel myself relax, let myself go rather than worrying that I'm taking too long, which has happened to me in the past.

I know I'm on the cusp of something big here and I start to shamelessly push myself against his mouth. He stills me with the palm of one hand, adds another finger inside me and increases the pressure with his lips and tongue and it drives me right over the edge. I think my eyes actually roll back in my head as I moan again, and surrender to what might be one of the best orgasms of my life.

When I open my eyes a moment or two later, struggling to get my breath back under control, he's watching me intently. "How was that for you?" He asks innocently, struggling to conceal a smile.

"It was . . . passable," I say nonchalantly, raising myself up onto my elbows. "I'll give you a 4 out of 5 on TripAdvisor." I'm lying of course. I would give him 10 out of 5 if I could.

"I'll reluctantly accept that rating for now, but please accept my assurances that I will endeavour to turn that 4 into a 5." Joe lightly traces one of my nipples with a lazy finger and winks at me. Christ, he is hot as hell. I need to return the favour.

"Take those off," I order, indicating his boxer shorts. He grins, his eyes half closed as he immediately obeys and oh Jesus . . .

He's beautiful and he's hard and he groans as I take him in my mouth. And I'm aiming for a 5 out of 5 rating first time with this one.

Chapter 19

J oe

I'm still feeling the after-effects of our early morning antics a couple of hours later as I wander down to meet Sienna for another roadtrip. Despite my assurances to her that I haven't completely lived like a monk for ten plus years, it's still been a good while since I've been that intimate with someone else and, I can't lie, it felt really nice.

Sienna is just so easy to be around. I am incredibly attracted to her but I also feel comfortable with her. I don't feel like she needs me to impress her, and I'm surprised at myself at how much I've actually opened up to her already, or at all for that matter. I normally play my cards close to my chest but she's gradually forcing my hand, apparently without even trying.

She's already waiting for me. She's wearing a mint coloured strappy beach dress over a turquoise bikini, and has a bright pink flower clip pinned into her tousled blonde hair. She looks so pretty. I can't believe she's mine.

I shake my head to clear my own thoughts. She's not mine. This isn't like that.

Sienna glances up at me and breaks into a smile, waving me over. I try not to dwell too much on the memories from earlier, force myself not to imagine her lying naked in front of me again. It's surprisingly difficult. "What are you up to?" I ask as casually as I can, walking towards her.

"Just doing an inventory of the communal bookcase," she replies, sipping an orange juice, and indicating the shelves that guests can leave their unwanted books on after they've finished them. "I didn't download enough books onto my kindle for my holiday apparently so thought I'd see if I could find a physical book to read. Usually they're all duds but I'm hoping I'll find a hidden gem."

I nod, sitting down at a nearby table. "Yeah, usually it's just duplicate copies of the same 'classic', books you've already read, or downright trash," I agree, stretching out my legs while I admire her bare tanned shoulders.

"Shall we play holiday bookshelf bingo?" she asks, wiggling her dark eyebrows at me. I frown back, confused. This is UK Birthday Number 1 all over again.

She giggles. "Take a guess at what might be on these shelves and I'll tell you if it's there." She raises her arms and gives a dramatic flourish towards the bookcase, like a magician's assistant. "There's no prize but you get the joy of taking part!"

She's such an idiot. An adorable one though.

"Oh right, I get it." I think for a minute. "Well, there's got to be at least one Dan Brown book there surely," I decide.

She scans the shelves. "One copy of The DaVinci Code and as many as three copies of Angels & Demons." She doffs an imaginary cap in my direction. "Well played, good sir."

"Okay . . . Fifty Shades of Grey?"

She pulls out one of the books from that series, and holds it out to me with a skeptical eyebrow raised. "You gave your copy away?" she jokes and I make a face at her. "Okay, you're batting two for two so far. Any other ideas?"

I correctly guess a Twilight book, a random self help book that clearly came free with a magazine bought at the airport, and a mostly used puzzle book will all be in that bookcase.

"Who does that?" Sienna wonders in disgust, thumbing through the puzzle book. "They've filled in every single puzzle, apart from the sudokus. What a psychopath." She shakes her head, placing it back on the shelf as I watch her, amused. "Ah... I think I've found the hidden gem!" She exclaims, sounding delighted all of a sudden.

She pulls another book out and scans the back. "It is what I thought it was! I've not read this in years. Did you ever read this?"

Before she even holds it up towards me, I recognise it.

She starts babbling excitedly about it, telling me the plot. It's about a nerdy guy in his late teens who one day discovers he can read minds... "you know, a bit like 'What Women Want' but without all the misogyny", but even that can't help him get the girl of his dreams.

"Yeah, I remember it," I say faintly.

I should be happy she thinks so much of it. Wait, no, I am happy about that. I'm over the moon, in fact.

Because remember that bestselling novel I mentioned I wrote years ago? That's the book she's currently waving around in her hand and raving about.

I just don't really want her to know that.

Chapter 20

Sienna

Joe seems a bit off today.

He didn't at first. I'd had a worry there might be a wee bit of awkwardness between us given the last time we'd been together we'd both had no clothes on, but actually my fears over that were unfounded. I can't pinpoint the moment that changed. Maybe he really didn't like me implying he was a secret fan of Fifty Shades?

So now we're in the car and I'm trying frantically to think of something to say that isn't cheese-related, just to break the awkward silence. I can't think of anything.

We pass a church and I grasp onto the first anecdote that comes into my head in relation to that. "Do you know the first thing my family used to do when we went on holiday to a new place? Look for the nearest Sunday Mass so we didn't miss a week." I grin at the memory.

"Once we had to travel fifty miles on a Sunday morning, except my dad got lost and we still missed the service. He was furious. "

"Ah the joys of a Catholic childhood," Joe says dryly. "I know it well myself; my parents were very religious." He catches my sidelong surprised glance and interprets it correctly. "Hey, just cos they mostly hated their kids, and each other, doesn't mean they needed to hate God too," he deadpans. I snort, despite myself.

At least that breaks the tension.

He starts to laugh. "What was that?" He asks as I feel my face flush pink. I suppose I should be grateful it was a snort and not a fart. "You sounded like a tiny pig."

"Sorry." I find myself giggling. "Sometimes I snort. I have no control over it."

He glances at me, and there's that look again. Eyes soft, slightly confused smile. "It was cute," he says quietly.

I feel like my insides are curling in on themselves. I want him to always look at me like that. It's sweet and intimate and just makes me feel . . . . special. Like he actually likes me, that this isn't just a physical thing.

But it also makes me feel scared.

I came on holiday thinking (somewhat overdramatically I admit) that my life was over and I'd never be happy again. But from pretty much the moment I met Joe I've felt . . . Alive.

I've never really been a fan of the whole "best way to get over a man is to get under another" adage - I'm more the type of person who has to go through a long mourning period before I would even consider another guy or relationship- but Joe has definitely broken through my defences on this occasion.

The problem is, I don't think he wanted to do that. I know he is not looking for a relationship, even though there's no doubt our chemistry is off the chart. He's dropped so many hints about this that I would have to be completely delusional to have missed them. He doesn't see this going anywhere. Which is a bit of a headfuck, granted, but at least I know it's nothing personal to me.

Unfortunately my heart is already getting involved, even while my head is screaming "don't do it!". Was there ever a chance I wouldn't start to develop feelings for Joe? That the lust I felt from that first glance wouldn't grow into something stronger once I started to get to know him?

I'm such a pathetic sap.

And, unfortunately, that sweet look on his handsome face just makes me want him more. Because he looks at me like I'm a secret he wants to keep to himself. And that then makes me wonder if maybe he might actually reciprocate these feelings I'm starting to have.

Thinking like that is edging me into a dangerous territory and I need to back the fuck out of it.

"Hey, do you mind checking Google maps on your phone and making sure I'm going in the right direction for Xi Beach?" Joe brings me back out of my confused brain.

"Sure." I welcome the distraction, pulling the app up quickly. "Looks like we're on the correct road so you're all good."

"Cool, thanks." He nods. "Is it just me or do some of these roads remind you of being in the Highlands?"

"Yes!" I'd been thinking this too. "I mean, it would have to be a rare sunny day in Scotland for them to look completely alike obviously but the similarities are uncanny."

Of course, talk of Scotland reminds me that we only have a couple of days left in Kefalonia and that our time together is finite; and that casts a shadow over my heart again because I'm falling for a guy I can only have on a temporary basis.

It takes less than an hour to reach Xi Beach but by this point I'm more than ready to exit the car; I feel like I need a bit of space to clear my head.

"It's not as red as the photos implied," Joe comments as we spread our towels out on the sand.

I agree. "But it's still pretty."

"Yep." He turns around and squints at me as the sun is in his eyes. A smile warms up his chiselled features. "Really pretty."

A warm glow consumes me. It's clear he's not talking about the beach.

And there he bloody goes again, making me feel all the things. Putting butterflies in my tummy, riling them up so they won't stop anxiously fluttering.

"You want a drink?" He asks. I nod. He wanders away to fetch me one.

I heave a sigh and take the book out of my bag. I was so happy to find it in the bookcase as I'd forgotten about its existence; I used to have a copy of it but I let someone borrow it years ago and it was never returned to me. I can't remember who I gave it to and I suddenly think wouldn't it be funny if this was the same copy, that had found its way back to me all those years later.

I know it's a ridiculous thought but I think it's probably already clear that I am indeed ridiculous.

The book is called "Thought Clouds". Apparently the guy who wrote it actually went to the same university as me. My friend Mel insists we even were in a lecture with him in our second year, although she can't remember which one. Some of our lectures did have hundreds of folk in them so I guess it's possible.

There's something nagging away at me though, as I stare at the book. It's like a tiny piece of a puzzle is missing in my brain and I can't quite find the piece needed to slot it all together.

Then I realise what the missing piece is. It's the author's name, printed in small type on the bottom right hand side of the front cover.

J.P. Quinn.

My brain goes into meltdown. Surely not? I think back to earlier in the bar, trying to pinpoint the exact moment that Joe's whole demeanor changed. It was somewhere around the point when I'd pulled this book off the shelf and started raving about it.

With shaking hands, I open the book and find the "about the author" page.

J.P. Quinn was born in Glasgow in 1987.

That's all I need to read to know.

Joe is J.P. Quinn?

The guy who kissed me senseless last night, who was naked with me this morning, who I'm trying so bloody hard not to fall for, wrote one of my favourite novels?

Fucking hell.

Chapter 21

Joe

Since I returned to our towels with two cans of Coke, I'm very aware of the fact that Sienna has been looking at me weirdly. I'm not sure why though. She has also barely spoken, which is really unlike her. She generally seems to see a silence as a challenge that she needs to fill.

I'm really not sure what's going on but I'm struggling with the silence myself now.

"I'm going to go for a swim," I eventually say, standing up and removing my t-shirt. I'm secretly hoping she might join me, that we could recreate that Myrtos Beach moment from yesterday, this time with the missing kiss, but she barely reacts.

"Enjoy," she says faintly. I can still feel her gaze on me as I walk towards the water though, burning into my back, hotter than the sun.

A few minutes later she materialises next to me in the sea and she seems to be back to normal. Actually, no, I take that back. She has what can only be described as her horny face on, that expression she wore on her face last night when she was telling me how hot she found my glasses. She looks downright predatory. She's like a different person when she goes into this mode and I can't deny it's unbelievably hot.

She winds her arms around my neck. And then her legs wrap around my waist. She stares at me, her eyes blazing, and then leans forward and lightly tugs on my bottom lip with her teeth.

Everything springs to attention at that. And I mean everything.

"Hey," she giggles, the one syllable word elongating into something longer and far more suggestive, leaving me in no doubt that she can feel how aroused I am. Not that I could have doubted it given that there's only two bits of flimsy material separating us. We may as well be naked. I wish we were.

She runs one hand down through the stubble on my jaw, gazing intently into my eyes, and that's when I snap, grasping the back of her neck to pull her closer and angling my lips onto hers. I breathe a sharp surprised gasp against her mouth though as she starts to subtly rub herself against me.

35 years old and I'm getting dry-humped in the Ionian Sea like a horny teenager. To be fair that would probably have been teenage me's fantasy. And a girl who looked like Sienna would likely have featured in that fantasy too.

"We'd better cool it," I pull back and whisper in her ear after a couple of minutes of this. "I know we're in the sea but we aren't exactly wearing invisibility cloaks."

"Fair enough," Sienna concedes. She's about to untangle her body from mine but I find I don't want her to go just yet. And so I grab her to pull her closer again, and slip a finger into her bikini briefs

She stills, taking in a sharp breath, and I watch her pupils dilating further as I move the finger against her. "Oh. My. God," she murmurs, pressing her mouth to mine again. She clings onto me, adjusting her position slightly to give me more access. "What are you doing to me?" she hisses a moment later, bending her head and nipping at my shoulder. "That feels incredible. "

"Good," I say quietly. "Just enjoy it." I want to watch her let go. I'm desperate to give her a second orgasm, one wasn't enough. Her reaction earlier was addictive. She's like a drug.

And we haven't actually even had sex yet.

I can feel her shaking, feel everything building up inside her. And then she's clenching around my finger, moaning "holy fuck, Joe" into my neck to try and smother too much tell-tale noise before she goes limp around me.

I can feel her panting against my skin for a moment or two, trying to control her breathing. Then she unwinds her limbs from around me and a shy smile lights up her flushed face. She's absolutely glorious.

"That," she says slowly. "Was amazing." And with that she flops back so she's floating on her back in the sea. She nudges me with one of her tiny feet. "Float with me. We can hold hands and pretend to be otters."

This girl is off her head.

And I'd be lying to myself if I said I'm not already nuts about her.

Chapter 22

Sienna

Well, that went a bit awry.

My plan, if you could even call it that, when I followed Joe into the water, was to confront him about the book. But I took one look at his face, into those wide green eyes, his wet dark lashes spiking together, and I suddenly couldn't even formulate words anymore. I longed to touch him, wrap myself around him, be wrapped in him. I couldn't think. I just wanted to feel.

And then I'd ended up having my first public orgasm.

Now that I was definitely not expecting. You know that episode of "Friends" where Rachel says the most interesting place she's ever had sex is the foot of the bed? I have never even been that adventurous before. Shagging with the lights on has probably been me at my most outrageous.

Somehow I have a feeling Joe has probably had sex in many more daring places. I bet he's done it on a beach before, for example. He's probably a fully paid up member of the Mile High Club too, whereas I can't understand how you can possibly fit more than one person in an aeroplane toilet, let alone do anything else.

Now the high I experienced in the sea is starting to wear off, I'm beginning to retreat back into my head, and my brain is rapidly filling to the brim with self-doubt now. And it's because of the memories of Joe - sorry, J.P. - that are starting to come back to me from all those years ago.

J.P. Quinn was actually a bit of a celebrity for a couple of months after the book was released; I hadn't been able to place Joe before now but that's clearly why he'd felt so familiar to me right at the beginning. I recall seeing photos of him in gossip mags such as Heat 13 or 14 years ago, and sure enough, the pictures were from events like premieres and after parties. Obviously, my memory has clung onto this somewhere in its depths when I'd felt like those were the sort of events he be-longed at. Because he actually had.

He wasn't quite as good-looking back then. More cute than handsome, a bit gangly and awkward. Turns out when I'd described my version of a younger him last night, I'd actually pretty much hit the nail on the head

- I'd just been a few years out due to his apparent transformation from self-proclaimed angry nerd.

J.P. had made a good celebrity. He'd been charming, I remember. Had an easy answer to any question thrown at him. Popular with the ladies as well. Those aforementioned magazine photos occasionally featured at least one stunning girl at his side.

It may already be obvious to you all, but turns out I actually did have a crush on the younger Joe, just like I imagined I would. It's just that he was J.P. back then, and I hadn't made the connection.

I think back all those years to that crush and remember at the time I was in (shocker!) a crappy relationship with a guy who was pretty much permanently stoned and had no energy or inclination to even leave his flat most of the time. J.P. seemed to be my boyfriend's polar opposite and I had wondered what it would be like to date him. Not that he would have been interested in me back then.

And now I'm already wondering why someone like Joe, who has just got better over time, would be slumming it with me, a recently dumped desperado, even just as a holiday fling. I feel like he could do so much better than me.

At the same time, I can't doubt the sincerity on his face when he confessed he'd been attracted to me since he saw me stepping on that bus. Or the lust that often seems to turn his eyes dusky when he looks at me. And let's not forget that sweet expression that seems to just say "I really really like you" and warms my insides like I've just downed a shot of tequila.

I'm struggling to process all of this. I know that Joe and J.P. are one and the same. But my brain is not quite able yet to sync up the former celebrity crush I'd practically forgotten about (I had a lot of celebrity crushes and his fame was fleeting) from 14 years ago with my current gorgeous holiday buddy who is very much present in my mind all of the time at the moment.

The early afternoon sun beats down on us. I shoot a glance at Joe, who is lying on his towel next to me, his eyes closed. He seems completely relaxed and at-ease, while I'm abuzz with nervous energy and questions. So many questions. Some of which I don't feel I can ask.

I'm going to have to tell him that I know though. If I don't, I think I'll go mad.

But maybe, my twisted mind thinks, maybe I'll have a bit of fun with the secret first . . .

Chapter 23

Joe

"Joe," Sienna whispers. "Are you awake?"

Of course I am. My brain won't switch off to allow me to relax enough to sleep. It keeps flipping between two thoughts: what I hope Sienna and I can do later now I've acquired some condoms (I didn't think to bring any with me given I had no plans for a holiday romance; thankfully my brother had loads), and the fact I noticed my book lying on her beach towel once I returned to the sand.

And the fear that if she makes the connection to me writing that book and realises the sort of dick I was back then, that the first thought may no longer be an option.

I'm not that guy anymore. Haven't been for a long time. I wasn't even that guy then really, I just got caught up in all that hype.

Now I think about it, are these fears proving I am that guy? I don't actually need the sex; I just don't want her to look at me differently, think of me as a different person.

I really hope I look more relaxed than I'm feeling inside because my stomach is churning with nervous energy right now.

"Joe?" she hisses again.

I suppose I've already proven I'm no good at faking sleep after the nip-slip incident, so I open my eyes to find her face close to mine, navy blue eyes sparkling with a strange energy. "You okay?" I ask.

She holds up a tube of suncream. "Was just wondering if you could do my back?" She says, her voice deliberately innocent. "I don't want to burn."

"Of course." I sit up. Any excuse to touch her.

She rolls onto her front and releases the tie at the back of her bikini. "I don't want a tan line," she explains. Then she props herself up on her elbows and, as I start to rub the cream into her shoulders, she opens her book. My book.

"I'm so glad I found this book," she says happily. My hands falter. "Do you know one of the things I liked most about it? I felt like the heroine looked a lot like me. I know that sounds crazy."

"Really?" I ask faintly. Also a bit confused. The main female character in my book has brown hair and brown eyes. So yes, it does sound a wee bit crazy.

"Yeah." She giggles. "I'm not a natural blonde, believe it or not. I'm brunette, I dyed my hair after I left uni and realised that blondes do have more fun. Or at least I did as a blonde." She flips a page over. 'The main girl in this book, Amy, has brown hair and freckles like mine. She also seemed to think a bit like me too. She didn't have the same colour of eyes obviously but I really identified with her. I really wanted to be her friend. You know, if she was real." She laughs again, self-deprecatingly.

"I understand that," I say quietly, squeezing cream out of the tube onto her back. God, her skin is so bloody smooth. I move my hands over her, working the sun-cream in. I could do this all day, although I'd really prefer the conversation to be about something else. She falls silent for a few minutes and I'm hoping that's the subject dropped.

"I've been trying to remember what the author was like," she says suddenly. Oh great, so we're still on the subject, and now the territory is even more dangerous. "You said you read it, right? Do you remember? I'm sure he ended up pretty famous for a bit."

"Hmmm," I pretend to think. "Nah, can't say I do," I reply eventually.

"He went to my uni," she volunteers. "At the same time as me."

I did?

"I'll maybe just Google him later," she says airily. "I don't seem to have a signal here." She sighs. "That feels so good. Are you sure you're not a secret masseuse?"

Nope. My secret is not that.

"There, I think that's you done," I announce, recapping the tube and moving back onto my own towel.

"Thanks Joe." She smiles at me, but there's an odd look on her face. She turns back to the book and seems intent on reading now. I feel myself starting to relax.

"What's your middle name?" She asks suddenly.

You'd think I'd be used to Sienna's random questions by now but she still always takes me by surprise. "Why?" I ask nervously. There's a weird edge to her voice.

She rolls onto her side and her smile widens. "I'm just wondering what the P in your name stands for," she replies. She closes the book and pointedly indicates the author name.

Fuck.

It appears Sienna is already on to me.

Chapter 24

Sienna

The moment of truth.

At first I think Joe's going to deny it, pretend he doesn't know what I'm talking about as he freezes at my words. Then he clears his throat and looks away. "Patrick," he mutters eventually, defeatedly. "My middle name is Patrick."

He drags a hand across his face and chances a glance back in my direction. "How long have you known?" he asks.

"I only just worked it out before I came to join you in the water," I say. "Why the big secret?"

He ducks his head, winces. Surprisingly, bashful is a good look on him. "I - um - don't know. I was . . . embarrassed."

"You're a freaking bestselling author, Joe! That's something to be so proud of. If I was in your shoes I'd be singing it from the rooftops."

He sighs, sounding a bit frustrated, lying down on the towel again and throwing a hand over his face. "That's not really the reason I didn't tell you," he bites out. "If you remembered who I was . . . I didn't want you to see me like that."

"I do remember you though," I'm so puzzled at his reaction. "As soon as I realised you were J.P. Quinn, I remembered exactly who you were from back then. It's funny though, I always assumed your name was John Paul."

"It's a logical assumption," Joe shrugs, sitting up again. "And a common misconception I never corrected. It ended up being a kind of . . . personna for me, I guess." He frowns broodily. "When I was J.P. I could do what I wanted, or so I thought."

I need to know more. But I feel like maybe we need a bit of truth serum here. Because right now I'm still failing to see why this was such a big secret for him. "Will we go get a drink? An alcoholic one?" I ask.

He doesn't hesitate. "Yes. But can we take the car back first? And put this conversation on hold for now?" He looks at me, sea green eyes clear and honest. "I will tell you everything, I promise. Even though you're going to probably think I'm a giant arsehole."

I nod. "Deal. About putting the conversation on hold, not about the arsehole thing. I'll reserve judgement on that for now," I hasten to add and he can't help but grin.

I paper over what otherwise would probably have been silence on the journey back to Lassi, filling it with my inane chatter while Joe mainly wears a forced smile and engages when required. After we've dropped the car off at the apartments we head down to one of the beach bars and I order the biggest carafe of wine I can. "Right, spill," I demand after I've poured us both massive glasses of white.

Joe throws half the glass of liquid down his throat and leans forward, pinching the bridge of his nose, clearly wondering where to start. "Okay, so I already told you I didn't exactly have the easiest of childhoods. I didn't have many friends, it's not that I was shy, I was just quite awkward back then. I think because my folks weren't really interested in me, I thought I didn't really have anything to offer anyone, that no one would really care what I had to say." My heart breaks a bit at that. "Even now, old habits die hard. I tend to get information out of other people but withhold a lot of my own."

He sighs. "You may have guessed I don't talk about this very often so this is a bit difficult for me. I suppose I've kind of compartmentalised my life into the pre-book file, then the famous author file, and then everything that happened since, and I try not to dwell on the first two files."

I nod supportively. "That makes sense," I agree. Although it doesn't really. Not yet anyway.

"I started writing 'Thought Clouds' when I was close to finishing school. I always felt I was better at expressing my thoughts in writing, and I didn't have to worry about boring anyone because it was just for me. I'd been writing stories for years; I've even got a whole Lord of the Rings type story I spent most of my teenage years on." He blushes, which is adorable. "I think I really thought I was going to be the next Tolkien for a bit, it's got maps and appendices and everything."

I smile. "I'd like to see that." I genuinely would. I really like it when he opens up. I'm also a massive Lord of The Rings fan but that's unrelated.

"You're literally the only other person who even knows of its existence. I've never told anyone else," he admits. His eyes meet mine for a long moment before they slip away and I feel those butterflies inside me resurrect themselves. "So I used to wonder whether my life would be different if I could read minds, if my own reactions and personality would be different. And that's how 'Thought Clouds' came about.

"I worked on it for a good few years. My own experiences would inspire a lot of the events of the book, and they'd sometimes change the course of the storyline too. And my female main character Amy changed too; originally she'd started off based on a girl I fancied in high school who I knew would never be interested in me, but then she ended up turning into another girl I'd often spot from afar and was intrigued by. I eventually finished it and editing it while I was still at uni but I had no intention of actually doing anything with it."

"So what changed?" I ask.

His lips curl upwards but it's a sad smile. "Tale as old as time," he says quietly. "I fell in love."

Ah.

Chapter 25

Joe

I met Sam when I was 20. She ended up sitting next to me in a lecture one day. I can't remember how exactly we started talking, but we immediately just hit it off.

I plucked up the courage to ask her out, and she accepted. As far as I'm aware she was the first girl who had ever been interested in me. I quickly fell head over heels and I was delighted to offload my virginity on her.

For some reason, Sam seemed fascinated by me, which I definitely wasn't used to, especially as it felt to me like she was way out of my league. So I found myself doing my best to entertain her, impress her. I was so unused to having attention and although I wasn't comfortable with it at first, I found I started to crave it; finally someone thought I was interesting. I eventually told her about the story I'd wrote and unsurprisingly she asked if she could read it.

She loved it, encouraged me to submit it to agents . . . And I found one. There was a bit of a bidding war and, just after I finished uni, the book was released.

And Sam was there for me the whole time, supporting me, reassuring me when I had regular bouts of imposter syndrome. Helping me deal with that initial onset of fame once it became clear my book was heading into bestseller territory. She was a great girlfriend.

"I didn't deserve her," I tell Sienna now. "And I quickly proved that."

"What did you do?" she asks, her eyes wide. She tops up our wine glasses.

I grimace. "I let fame go to my head. There was this model at the time, Leesa Meadows?" She nods in recognition. "She'd approached me at a couple of events, and she was definitely keen. And, I was 22 and she was hot... I can't even defend my actions. I ended up cheating on Sam with her. Sam would see photos of me at events and ask about Leesa but I would lie and say our PR folk just wanted us to present a united front, etc etc. All bullshit, of course.

"At this point, I wasn't even sorry. I just . . . It was like I thought I deserved this now, I'd had a crappy childhood so now this was my reward. In my head, I almost put the blame on Sam for getting me into this situation, for encouraging me. Like I said, I was a dick."

"Did Leesa know you had a girlfriend?" Sienna's face is hosting a mix of emotions right now. It's difficult to tell which one is prevailing. I know my story won't be endearing me to her though, especially with her recent history. Which was precisely what I wanted to avoid in all of this.

I nod in answer to her question. "She did. I don't think she really cared at first. But then I was spending more time down in London by that point, and she was there too and Sam was back in Glasgow so we got a lot closer . . . And at some point I told her me and Sam were over. But we weren't. I was planning to end it because we were going in two different directions, but I just hadn't been able to bring myself to do it yet." A sharp bitter laugh I wasn't expecting bursts out of my mouth. "The irony of it all was that I didn't want to hurt her."

"Wow," Sienna whispers, almost to herself. She looks up. "Oh sorry, go on!" She waves to me to continue.

"So I'm juggling these two girls, feeling simultaneously smug and disgusted with myself, with smug mostly winning out admittedly, when I'm approached to go on a reality TV show."

Her eyes brighten with recollection at this. "Oh yes, so you did. It was like a version of Celeb Big Brother but on a satellite channel, right? I didn't have the channel but I saw some coverage of it in magazines at the time."

"Yeah. It was a crock of shit, frankly. But my agent thought it would be good for a bit of extra publicity for the book, and my ego was so big by that point that it practically needed its own hotel room. I was more than happy to do the show at the time. This was my chance to finally prove to all the folk who had ignored me growing up that I was actually worth something." I glance over at Sienna. "Do you remember what happened?"

She shakes her head slowly, clearly thinking. "There's a vague memory of some sort of scandal involving you; I can't remember what it was though."

I sigh. "Dickhead here struck again. There was a young pretty soap actress also on the show, Cecilia, and of course I couldn't resist getting to know her a bit better. Despite the fact I was still seeing Sam and Leesa. And despite the fact I was on camera the whole fucking time. It's true what they say, you know: you do forget you're being filmed."

"Did you . . . You know?" Sienna asks, wide-eyed. I shake my head.

"Oh god, no! We didn't progress beyond kissing really. There was a bit of a steamy hot tub session but that was it." I cringe at the memory. "Anyway, ratings weren't that great so the producers decided to shake things up a bit, they'd schedule in some visits from our loved ones.

"To be honest, I assumed they meant family and I knew they wouldn't show up. Not even Jack - I knew he had no interest in being on TV. So I wasn't actually expecting anyone. But . . .,"

"Fuck, yes, I remember what happened now!" Sienna almost shouts in excitement. "Oops, sorry." She calms herself down. "They brought both your girlfriends in at the same time to confront you while you sat there with your arm around the actress, right?"

"It was literally one of the worst moments of my life," I say wearily. "At that moment I was just confronted with what an absolute arsehole I'd become. Sam was devastated, Leesa was spitting feathers, Cecilia was just mortified as she hadn't realised she was stepping on anyone's toes . . . And I couldn't even defend my actions. Unsurprisingly, I was the first so-called celebrity to be voted out of the show by the public after that. And funnily enough, none of the girls wanted anything to do with me."

"Goodness." Sienna's voice is faint.

I nod grimly. "So yeah, when you ask why I didn't want to tell you who I really was? It's because I didn't want you to remember any of that."

Now I just have to hope she doesn't judge me too harshly.

Chapter 26

Sienna

Joe looks wrecked by the time he's finished telling his tale. And I have to admit I feel a bit knackered too from listening.

I'd completely forgotten about that terrible reality TV show, about all the publicity J.P. Quinn and his three-timing ways had generated at the time. Half the UK, mostly male, thought he was a hero. The other half, mostly female, thought he was a twat.

"What did you do after the scandal?" I ask Joe. "You pretty much disappeared after that."

"I went travelling," he replies. "I needed to get away, clear my head. Be where people didn't know who I was and what a massive tit I'd made of myself. Luckily it was only really in Britain that I was recognised. I had made a decent amount from my book and other things I'd done

- like that show - and in an amazing feat I hadn't twatted it away so I was okay for money. And I started getting a lot of freelance gigs doing travel articles so I was able to stay away for a long time. I didn't go back to London for five or six years and by that time, thankfully, everything had blown over."

"And the relationship thing, the fact you don't do them?" I prompt. "This is because of that?"

He nods. "Pretty much. I know I really hurt those girls. And although I know I'm not that same guy now, it's always played on my mind that maybe, presented with that same scenario, I'd do it again. So it's been easier for me to just not get attached." I can't help but notice his eyes seem sad though.

I can't help reaching out to touch his hand. "For the record, Joe," I say softly, "I definitely don't think you're that guy anymore."

He glances up at me, his forehead wrinkling adorably. "It means a lot that you think that. I thought you'd hate me, especially after what happened with your ex."

I shake my head. "Look, it clearly wasn't your finest hour. But I'm not going to compare something you did 13 years ago when you were practically still a kid to a 37 year old man's actions. And you're clearly still pun-ishing yourself for what you did, whereas Greg probably doesn't even give me a second thought."

"I think you're wrong about that." Joe puts his other hand on top of mine, green eyes searing intensely into me. "He probably regrets losing you every single day. And if he doesn't, he's even more of a fucking idiot than I thought."

My breath catches in my throat at his words. The way he's looking at me right now makes me want to throw myself on him. Despite everything that he's told me. Or maybe because of? Once again, I feel like he's letting me in, possibly in a way he never has with anyone before.

And, forgive me for being crude, but it makes me want to let him in. To me. *wink wink*

Let the holiday buddies become the holiday fuck buddies.

"Thanks." My voice comes out in a rasp. I clear my throat, embarrassed. "That means a lot to me too." I stand up. "Oh and by the way, we only have two more days here so you're not going to have much opportunity to cheat on me anyway." I resort to a joke, feeling awkward. "Will we go get something to eat?"

He's looking at me a bit strangely now but nods after a brief hesitation. "Sure," he murmurs. "Let's go."

By the time we've both hungrily devoured burgers, we're definitely feeling the after effects of the sun, the wine and Joe's confession. "How about we grab another bottle of wine from the shop and head back to my apartment?" I ask. Kate has already text to tell me she'll once again be staying with Jack. "We can watch the sunset from the balcony."

And then... who knows!? I know what I want to happen though!

"Sounds like a plan."

On the balcony I pour our wine into tumblers and break open a big bar of Milka chocolate. In companionable silence, we watch the sky turning various shades of pink and red as the sun dips beyond the horizon, Joe's arm draped around me, pulling me close. I'm suddenly aware of just how happy I am in this moment, with my beautiful surroundings and this incredible guy at my side.

I don't want it to end.

"I like you so much," Joe breathes suddenly, into my ear. Goosebumps erupt onto my skin. I turn to face him and his face is as serious as it was last night, just before that first glorious kiss. I cup his face in my hands and brush his lips with my own before I can stop myself. We haven't kissed since Xi Beach and it's as if I've forgotten how addictive it is.

"I like you so much too," I echo, feeling his stubble prickling against my palms as I lean in for another kiss. Smiling, he tugs me to my feet and leads me back inside, to the bed.

We do nothing but kiss for a long time. It might be hours, it might be minutes, I have no idea. Time has ceased to exist, nothing matters but us. Gradually, eventually, we start to pull at clothes, and his lips move down to my neck. "I want you so badly," he whispers between kisses. "You have no idea, Sienna."

I know how wet I am before he even touches me there, how ready I am for him. "I stole some condoms from Jack's stash," he chuckles as I hear him tear a wrapper open. "Don't tell him."

And then he's inside me fully and we're moving together and oh my god it feels like we fit together perfectly. His eyes widen as he looks into mine, as if in shock, as if he realises this too.

"Fuck," he bites out, lowering his face to mine to kiss me again, one hand slipping back between my legs so he can tease me at the same time. Oooh, so we're going for at least three orgasms for me today then?

I can live with that.

In the end I give in slightly before he does, still contracting around him as he succumbs too, hissing my name into my neck. We lie together, gathering ourselves for a moment before we lock eyes again. I can hear both of our hearts pounding.

"Well," Joe says finally, his voice soft and husky. "I don't know about you, but I'm definitely going to want to do that again."

I agree wholeheartedly.

Chapter 27

Joe

We first met on Friday evening and now it's Monday morning. I can't believe how much has happened in that time. How easily Sienna has worked her way under my skin.

Those first two days I spent with Sienna went by unbelievably slowly in relation to the next two days.

Our last two days together.

From Monday though, things jump into high gear. We leave on Wednesday morning and everyone knows the last couple of days of a holiday always fly in. You want to hold onto them, make them last, but you sadly have no control over them.

On Monday morning, we're both a little hungover, sunburned and exhausted from spending a lot of the night awake. Although it doesn't stop us repeating the antics of the previous night, obviously.

I have the car until Tuesday morning so once we have recovered from our sore heads, I suggest we go to Argostoli. "We can drive over and leave the car there. I can run and get it in the morning."

"Oh, so you're a runner?" Sienna asks, raising her eyebrows admiringly as she blatantly perves on my body. "That explains a lot."

"Stop it." I can't help but smile though. I like her ogling me. "Just to warn you, the walk back from Argostoli is pretty steep."

"I'm sure I can manage," Sienna says airily. "I've been to the gym at least three times in the last six months."

We head to Argostoli via the coast road as I have a feeling Sienna will like the lighthouse on the way.

I was right. "Oh, this is seriously cool," she says, after we've parked nearby and wandered up the man-made peninsula to where the white structure lies at the water's edge. It's like no lighthouse I've ever seen, with its round structure and numerous columns but it's awesome.

"Look, I match!" Sienna poses in front of the building in her white strappy dress. She runs over with her phone. "Take a photo of me? I need to Instagram this shit."

"Of course." I snap one of her with her phone and then I can't resist taking one of her with my own phone. I need that memory of her leaning against one of the columns and smiling at me coyly to be real.

"That for the spank bank once you get home?" She asks me, grinning. "Oh Joe, if you need a photo, I'm sure I could do so much better than that." She winks as she grabs her phone back off me and wanders around the lighthouse to grab another picture of it from a different angle.

While I try desperately to control my libido.

Sienna has grabbed a couple of cans of Fanta Limon from her fridge before we headed out and we sit by the lighthouse in the bright sunshine and drink them, relaxing for a few minutes. Sienna lays her head on my shoulder contentedly and I find myself playing with her hair. "That's nice," she sighs. I press a kiss on her head too before I release her and we head back to the car. I'm very aware of the fact I'm acting like a boyfriend but I can't stop myself somehow.

I don't think I want to.

In Argostoli we wander over the De Bosset Bridge and back before Sienna spots pedalos. "Oh, we should hire one of those!" she exclaims excitedly. "I read some-where that you might see a giant sea turtle."

"Let's do it."

We head to the kiosk to hire one and set off through the water. "God, I'm tired of pedalling already," Sienna groans after about ten minutes. "And now I'm worrying that a sea turtle is going to appear right next to me and give me the fright of my life."

We drift along for a few moments, making sure we're not close to any land or other boats.

"So why did you move back to Glasgow?" Sienna asks suddenly, taking a sip from her bottle of water.

"I'm not sure really," I admit. "I just missed it. London was exhausting me; and it's always reminded me too much of . . . Well, you know, what happened."

"Ah," she nods. "How long ago did you come back?"

"Actually just before the pandemic."

"Did you manage to find freelance work easily during that?" she asks. Now I've unloaded my secrets on her, I don't mind all the questions as much.

"I found it pretty scarce unless I wanted to write about covid. And I didn't. But I was lucky that I had money and I own my flat outright. So I didn't have to actually find work."

"So what did you do instead?" She's flopped back against the seat and closed her eyes.

"I . . ." Why is this so difficult to say? "I actually ended up writing a sequel to 'Thought Clouds'."

"What?" She shoots upright. "You're kidding!"

I shake my head. "No joke. I was stuck in the flat, didn't have anything better to do. And suddenly, after not wanting to think of that book for so long, I found myself wanting to continue the story."

"That's amazing! And is it . . . Is it getting published?" Sienna gasps then laughs at herself. "Sorry Joe, I think I'm fangirling a bit over here right now!"

"Actually, yes. There's a press release going out about it. On Thursday." I swallow. "After we're back home."

I've been dreading this for weeks now. Months, even. Ever since I started writing that sequel, unable to stop myself. Knowing there was a chance my slightly murky past could come back to haunt me. Almost hoping it wouldn't be any good so that my agent, who had been bugging me for years to write another book, would laugh in my face after reading it. So that there would be no chance of it getting published.

"Are you okay about that?" Sienna asks astutely. I shake my head.

"Not really."

We start pedalling again and quietly I tell Sienna all my worries about potentially being in the spotlight again. She strokes my arm lightly and calms me down, talking me off my metaphorical ledge.

I feel ridiculously close to her at this point. Like I could tell her anything. She knows all the bad stuff already though, and seems to accept me for it.

We leave the pedalo and wander to a nearby restaurant, sitting next to the water with plates of feta baked in pastry and drizzled with honey, and of course a carafe of wine. Sienna picks up her glass and looks over the sea to the mountains with a contented sigh.

"I can't believe we didn't spot any giant sea turtles the whole time we were in the boat . . . and then saw one immediately on the other side of the bridge the second we walked away," she gripes a moment later.

I laugh. "You basically said you'd piss your pants if one appeared next to you on the boat, you should be relieved."

"That's true," she concedes. "They're cute but they also kind of scare me. A bit like E.T."

I nearly choke on my wine. "You're scared of E.T?"

She shrugs. "I mean, he's adorable, but if he just appeared beside you when you weren't really expecting him, you'd probably get a bit of a fright, right?"

I suppose she makes a good point.

After we've finished the feta and polished off the wine, we make a start on the aforementioned steep climb over the hill. "Shit, this is terrible!" Sienna cries, stopping for at least the third or fourth time in as many minutes.

"This is not the sort of exercise one should have to do on a relaxing holiday."

"I did warn you," I remind her.

"It just feels like this must be my punishment for having such a good time with you," she rues, and I find myself stopping as her words sink in. I realise, not for the first time, that it's been a long time since I've had so much fun. The last few days have been a revelation.

Sienna stops and turns, glancing at me impatiently before her eyes turn pleading. "Can you push me up the hill for a bit?" She asks. "Just shove my back for a minute or two."

I place one hand on the small of her back and start directing her up the rest of the hill, while struggling not to overthink things.

When we finally reach the top of the hill between Argostoli and Lassi, she pretends she's about to faint, then launches into some sort of victory dance. "I survived! You're my hero!" She declares dramatically before flinging her arms around me and smiling into my eyes. She is such an eejit.

I can't believe we only have one day left together.

Chapter 28

S ienna

 Tuesday morning.

It's my last full day with Joe and I'm not sure my brain is ready to accept it.

When he leaves to get the car from Argostoli I find myself already missing him which doesn't bode well. Maybe I should have ran with him? Wrung out every bit of time I possibly could with him?

Who am I kidding though; my whole body is sore just from walking up that hill yesterday, even if I could run there's no way I'd be able to do so today.

We've agreed a lazy day by the pool would be good after our adventures of the last few days, so I pack up my beach bag and head down to the pool while he's away, laying out his towel on the lounger next to mine and closing my eyes. I'm trying not to think of the time limit on our fling but I feel like there's a countdown flashing on the top right hand side of my vision, even when I close my eyes.

I must drift off to sleep though because when I wake up, he's sitting on his lounger, gazing into space. I can't help but smile that he's back. "You okay?" I ask curiously. He snaps out of his trance and nods vigorously.

"Absolutely.'

He grins at me but the smile doesn't quite meet his eyes. I reach out and squeeze his hand, tightly.

Kate and Jack appear not long after and join us. Is this officially about to be the longest my best friend and I have spent together all holiday? On the last day? God, I'm so glad I found Joe!

Joe and Jack head up to the pool bar for some booze (it's only 11am but it's our last day, give me peace!) and Kate turns to me. "So what's happening with you guys?" She asks nosily.

I screw up my face in response. "Holiday fling, that's all."

"You don't seem sure," Kate says keenly.

"In a perfect world, maybe it would be different." I try my best to be nonchalant. "But I'm barely over Greg and Joe isn't looking for a relationship so it's not going to work out."

"You just said you're 'barely over Greg'" Kate points out eagerly. "So you are over him?"

"Huh." I'm taken aback. I replay my own words in my head. "I guess I am."

The problem is I've just swapped one hopeless infatuation with another. And, much like I did with Greg, I've pretty much clung onto Joe like a life jacket. With Greg it was loneliness after initial lockdown that made me clasp on too tight; and now Joe has filled a similar type of metaphorical hole when Kate abandoned me here.

Anyway, I'm still on holiday and I don't want to over-think things. Let me just psycho-analyse myself tomorrow once I'm back home with only a blanket, rhubarb gin, and my tears to keep me company on the couch.

The brothers have returned from the bar. It's nice to see them laughing and joking with one another when I know their relationship hasn't always been easy. It must be hard to both go through the same experience with such different outlooks. Joe places a bottle of Kopparberg in my hand with a wink.

"Good choice, it's practically fruit juice," I praise him, taking a nice big gulp of it.

"Listen," he says quietly, presumably so Kate and Jack don't overhear. "I know this is going to sound a bit crazy as we've kinda been doing this anyway but since it's our last night together tonight . . . Can I take you on a date?"

"So what makes it different from what we've been doing already?" I ask blankly.

His green gaze focuses intently on me. "I'll actually plan something rather than us just saying 'let's meet in the pool bar at seven and we'll go from there'," he replies, dimples popping as a cheeky smile spreads across his face. "And maybe I'll even come and pick you up."

"How romantic," I tease. His smile slips momentarily then comes back somehow brighter.

"So what do you think?"

"Sure." I nod. I take another sip of my cider before placing it down on the ground next to my lounger and closing my eyes again.

Later I'm back in my apartment, make- up and hair already done, trying to decide what to wear, while also trying to re-pack my suitcase. Turns out living out of your suitcase is all fun and games until it's just a big tangled mass of wrinkled clothing. I finally locate the dress I've been hunting for, a violet lacy skater dress, and slip it on.

I'm feeling a sweaty, stressed mess as I hear a knock at the door, and I march over to open it, holding my sandals in my hand.

"Hey..." The words die on my lips and I drop my shoes as I look up at him. It's like I forget how handsome Joe is every time I'm away from him.

He's wearing jeans and a slim fitting black shirt, sleeves rolled up of course. (Mmmm, arms.) He's also already wearing his glasses. As my eyes linger lustfully, he pushes them up and says "my eyes are tired" in explanation. But he smirks as he says it and I know, just know, he's wearing them because he knows how much I like them.

Well played.

He holds out a bar of Milka and a bottle of prosecco. "I thought about bringing flowers but I somehow had a feeling you'd appreciate these more."

"You were right." I'm not a massive fan of flowers as a gift. I hold both items close to me and inhale deeply. "Oh Joe, they smell amazing," I joke, winking at him, and he laughs. "Let me see if I can find a vase." I slide them into the fridge and straighten up.

"You look gorgeous." He's studying me from head to toe as I turn back around. There's a new look in his eyes this time . . . The heat is there but so is the softness. "I want to fuck you senseless" combined with "but I really fucking like you too."

I'm melting and it's not just because of the excessively warm weather. "Thanks," I mumble, feeling myself blush under his appraisal. I sit down on the bed to fiddle about with my sandals. Why are the straps and buckles always so awkward? My hands suddenly feel like mittens and won't do what I want them to do.

"Let me help." He sinks to his knees in front of me and, before I can protest, grasps one of my ankles, easily slipping the strap through and securing it. His fingers lightly run along my foot for a moment and my breath catches at the touch.

He moves onto my other foot and quietly I observe him as he concentrates on his task, notice how long his lashes are behind the lenses of his glasses, that he's biting his full bottom lip. I inhale his cologne, which smells so fresh and just so him.

I'm so busy watching him that I don't even realise he's buckled me successfully into the other sandal too until he looks up and meets my gaze. "That's you sorted," he says softly, after a long moment. He rises gracefully to his feet. "Ready to go?"

"Definitely."

Because if we don't leave now I'm going to jump on you.

Chapter 29

Joe

For some reason it was really important to me that I take Sienna on a proper date.

I don't really know why.

That's a lie. I know exactly why. Because despite myself, I've caught feelings. Feelings I am struggling to shake or even quite understand yet. Ten plus years of "monk life" with only an occasional one night stand or short lived fling thrown in will do that to a person.

But I'm pretty sure, if I really dig under the surface - the way I've been trying so hard not to since that first moment I saw Sienna - that I'm starting to fall for her. That I don't actually want this to end.

That, for the first time in forever, since Sam, I've found someone I've allowed myself to get close enough to and actually bond with in order to even consider a relationship. Of course, that thought terrifies me too because the last thing I want to do is hurt Sienna the way I hurt Sam and I don't even know how to be in a relationship anymore. I've only really been in one with Sam and look how that turned out.

But Sienna makes me want to try. She challenges me and I just really like being around her. And I don't think I've developed feelings because of the scenario we've found ourselves in . . . I don't actually think I would have offered to keep her company all the time like this if I didn't already have that want for her festering. I'm a nice guy, but I'm not that nice.

It sounds cheesy as baked feta but it does feel a bit like fate threw us together, that it knew this was meant to happen.

As pretty much a lifelong cynic, it has taken me a lot to even admit this.

And as for the date itself? I wanted to put an official label on it to test myself. To see if it immediately put me into some sort of panicked tailspin.

It didn't. It hasn't.

Obviously, I don't know if Sienna even thinks there's any sort of future for us outside of this beautiful little Greek island we've both happened to find ourselves on at the same time. But if she does? Then maybe, just maybe, we can somehow make it work.

I take her to a cocktail bar on the main strip before dinner. "Why don't we choose each other a cocktail we think the other will like?" I suggest as we scan the menus. It seems like a little game that will be right up Sienna's street.

She looks nervous though. "What if I get it wrong and it's a waste of money?" she frets. I smile reassuringly, reaching out and stroking her arm.

"I have every faith in you."

We take turns to go up to the bar. I choose her a strawberry daiquiri, which according to her is exactly what she would have chosen. After a bit of deliberation she opts for a mojito for me.

"I assumed you like these because they're mentioned in the book," she says bashfully. She's spot on. At the time I started writing 'Thought Clouds" a mojito was the only cocktail I'd ever tasted. I thought it was the ultimate in sophistication at the time. I drank them a lot in my wanky, famous author days back then. I actually only recently re-started appreciating them.

It's only started occurring to me how much of my life I've put on hold thanks to my mistakes of years ago. And this realisation has also been because of the beautiful girl sitting opposite me, smiling anxiously as she waits for my verdict on her choice. She's forced me to face a lot of my demons.

"Good decision?" Sienna asks finally and I notice that I've just been staring at the drink without saying anything.

"Absolutely." I nod, take an emboldened sip (god, it's refreshing) and end up, of course, telling her about my self-imposed break from most things that reminded me of my past. It's actually so nice to be able to just be this honest with someone. I hadn't realised how much I've been holding back from anyone all of these years.

After cocktails we head to a restaurant that, according to several TripAdvisor reviews, has the best baked feta starter out of all the restaurants in the area. When I tell Sienna this she laughs and says "My expectations are probably too high now . . . but I'm excited."

It turns out it is pretty damn good - now I've been converted to the baked feta cause I of course have to try it too - and after white wine and mains we make our way back to our apartments.

But what to do next? I didn't get further in planning beyond drinks and dinner, not sure how long those would actually take. "I'd suggest the pool bar for a couple of drinks but the music they play is appalling," Sienna laughs as if reading my mind. "It's all weird covers of classic songs. Earlier they were playing a dance cover version of 'Creep' by Radiohead." She shakes her head.

We are nearly at the bar and the music starts to filter into our senses. "Wait, is that what I think it is?" I pause.

She also stops to listen. "If you're thinking it's a dance cover version of 'In the End" by Linkin Park, you'd be right. And I cannot listen to them butcher another classic like that." She clasps my hand tighter and pulls me past the bar. "Thank goodness you brought me that prosecco earlier. YouTube Roulette in the apartment it is!"

Time for another Sienna game.

She explains herself as she loads up YouTube on her phone and I open up the prosecco. "I'll randomly choose a song and after we've listened to it, you need to choose a song that comes up in the videos below that one, and so on. You can't just put a new song suggestion into the search box, it has to be on the screen for you to choose it. Make sense?"

I nod, removing the cork from the prosecco as she continues to fiddle about with her phone. "Okay, I've put it into incognito mode otherwise it'll probably just come up with suggestions of all the ridiculous songs I was listening to while I festered in heartbreak and that would be fucking mortifying."

She sits on her bed, leaning against the wall, and pats the space next to her, so I slip down beside her as the first song starts to play.

It's "Respectable" by Mel & Kim.

Sienna's blue eyes twinkle with mischief as she gives me a sidelong glance. "I hate you," I tell her.

"Oh come on, it's a great song," she smiles, nudging me and grabbing the bottle from my hand.

We sit in half-darkness, taking turns to swig prosecco directly from the bottle as we listen to different songs as part of Sienna's little game. I hear tunes I haven't heard in years like "Waiting For A Star to Fall" by Boy Meets Girl and Jermaine Stewart's "We Don't Have To Take Our Clothes Off."

I question the roulette element to the name of Sienna's game as I don't believe there is one but she just says "shut up, it's a fun name."

And to be fair, it's a fun game too. I'm having a blast.

It's my turn to pick another song and I'm scrolling through the options when a WhatsApp notification slides onto the screen. I don't have to open it to see who it's from or what it says, and my heart sinks into my stomach at the words appearing on the screen. Luckily, Sienna currently has her head in the fridge to retrieve the chocolate and doesn't hear my stifled groan.

Can we talk when you get back from your holiday? I miss you. X

The message, of course, is from her ex.

Chapter 30

S ienna

I can't help but take a moment to appraise Joe as I turn from the fridge to see him scrolling through my phone. A frown is slightly marring his handsome features, his glasses sliding down his long, straight nose. Broody is yet another good look on him. I stifle a sigh.

"Chocolate?" I offer, breaking off a piece of Milka and slipping it into my own mouth. He glances up, his eyes lingering on my lips, and then smiles and stands. The opening notes of what I think is "Rush Rush" by Paula Abdul (classic ballad) are drifting out of my phone, which he leaves on my bed as he walks towards me. He takes a square of chocolate himself, then holds out his hand.

"Dance with me?" he asks quietly. Slightly shyly, even. Intense green eyes are burning into mine and, as cheesy a move as it seems to be, I can't resist letting him pull me towards him, his warm arms wrapping around me. I hold him too, and rest my head against him, feeling his heart beating as we sway, somewhat self-consciously, along with the music. My breath quickens at the closeness, the intimacy, of this act.

I'm going to miss this guy so bloody much.

He pulls back after a moment so he can examine my face. "You okay?" he asks softly. His gaze is serious, as if he's searching my thoughts somehow. Maybe his book was based on reality after all and he can read minds? I don't think I want him to know what I'm thinking though; he'd probably run a mile.

I force a smile when really I feel more like crying. "Just can't believe we're going home tomorrow," I reply. "Time flies when you're having fun."

Joe nods. "That's true." He bends slightly to study my shoulder; it's exposed due to my dress having a bardot neckline. "I think something has bitten you," he remarks, touching the skin lightly with one finger.

"I'm a mosquito magnet," I explain, my voice catching. "I'm actually amazed I don't have more bites than that. They usually form a committee to welcome me off a flight."

He chuckles then presses his mouth carefully against my shoulder, the briefest of kisses. The tenderness of the gesture shoots arrows of lust straight down between my legs and I can't help the sigh that escapes my mouth. His eyes narrow thoughtfully as they return to my face. It's hard to decipher his expression. I wonder if he's okay.

Before I can consider this further, his lips find mine and all doubts fly out of my head. It's so gentle; no urgency at all, his tongue stroking mine, tasting of chocolate and alcohol. It makes my whole body ache for him. One hand moves to the back of my neck so he can manoeuvre my face closer to his, while the other remains on my back, his hand burning into the skin there as if branding me.

In this moment I realise something with absolute certainty, and it terrifies me.

In the space of four days I have somehow fallen completely in love with Joe Quinn.

For fucks sake, Sienna. You've really gone and done it this time haven't you?

This isn't just a holiday fling for me. This is it. He's the one.

And I couldn't feel more helpless and hopeless about it when he's made it clear that he doesn't want a relationship. With me or anyone else.

This realisation, quite frankly, is the last thing I wanted. Although fairly typical of my life, admittedly.

I rally though. I don't want to put any sort of downer on our last night together. Instead I channel my feelings, pretend to myself he feels the same, and lean right into the act.

Ramp up the passion level in the kissing. Steer us towards the bed, pushing him down onto it, unbuttoning his shirt, running my hands over his chest and abs, stroking my way along the trail of hair leading down below the waistband of his jeans until he gasps and rolls me over onto my back, his eyes dark with desire.

He stands briefly to remove his shirt fully, pull his jeans and boxers off, tossing his glasses to one side, before he helps me with my clothes, his hands and lips roaming everywhere in the process. It's like a switch has flipped and he's like a man possessed all of a sudden. And he's acting exactly how I need him to act, which makes it easier for me to pretend this is for real on both sides.

There's still music playing but I have no idea if I even recognise the songs, all I can feel is him, thrusting into me, biting my neck, toying with me with his fingers . . . My senses are completely taken up by Joe and nothing else. In that space of time, I couldn't care less about anything else.

Afterwards, he kisses me slowly again and lies down beside me, stroking my stomach as he drifts off to sleep.

I find myself wide awake, my eyes wet, wishing things could be different.

Once I'm sure he's definitely unconscious, I slip out of his arms and pull my pyjamas on. I still have some packing to do so I may as well distract myself with that. I also find the tiny purse I keep my Euros in, and transfer the currency into my normal purse, which is always full to the brim with too many random membership cards, old photos and usually too many coins. One time I even got stopped at security because of how much my purse was bulging in my bag. I learned my lesson after that.

Now that I'm thinking about it, I should really give my Euros to Joe; he has paid for most things for us this trip and it's really not fair. I'll speak to him about it in the morning. Sadness overwhelms me again.

Still unable to find sleep, I sit on the balcony with the remainder of the prosecco bottle. I close my eyes and curse my stupid heart for falling for someone who doesn't feel the same.

Sure, Joe likes me, and fancies me. I've let my guard down around him, allowed him to witness my silly side, my vulnerable corners, the random thoughts I some-times can't help but voice aloud. But he's only experi-enced a snapshot of what being with me is like. He'd be bored of me in no time, like Greg was, like previous boyfriends before him have been. The novelty value always wears off quickly, just like the sheen of a holiday does.

And let's circle back, for the seven millionth time, to the fact that he doesn't want to be in a relationship.

I sigh, rub my eyes and go back inside. My phone stopped playing music a long time ago and I pick it up, double-taking as I see Greg's name on my screen. What the fuck?

I briefly wonder if Joe saw the message from him, remembering that frown on his face just before he asked me to dance. Not that it really matters. I'm not getting back with Greg. I've no interest in talking to him either. That ship sailed when I realised he was cheating on me; I was never going back there anyway. And he might miss me, but I sure as hell don't miss him now.

He doesn't have the ability to break me anymore. That honour belongs to someone else now.

My gaze drifts over to Joe, snoozing so peacefully on my bed; so completely unaware that he's about to shatter my already fragile heart into pieces.

Chapter 31

Joe

Greg's text had definitely thrown a metaphorical curveball into my brain. Or maybe more of a gutterball as it made me realise that my thoughts of the possibility of a future with Sienna were probably pointless.

I had to remind myself that she herself was still heartbroken just a few days ago; she had even cried about him on our first meeting. How could I expect her to be ready to move on with someone else? With me, of all people? The guy who was once exposed on TV and to all the British tabloids as a three-timing cheater?

And I thought back to the day I told Sienna my sordid tale; she'd reassured me that she didn't believe I was that guy anymore but then within moments joked that I had only two days left with her so wouldn't have time to cheat anyway. I know her words were lighthearted but she'd made it pretty clear she only saw me as a fling.

So that's that really.

I walked over to her after seeing that message, wishing I had those superpowers from my book as I looked into her eyes. What was she thinking? Should I tell her there was a message from her ex on her phone? I decided against it; I didn't want another guy on her mind. Not in that moment.

As I lie in bed next to her in the early hours of the morning, as she sleeps soundly beside me, I reflect on the previous night. For me, at least, it all felt real. But I'm going to have to dust myself off and move on.

Maybe I'm finally ready for a relationship after all; but right now I can't picture that scenario unless it has Sienna Norton in it.

The airport transfer is an early one; pick-up is just after ten am so we don't have much time to chat once we get up. Everything is a bit of a blur: checking that belongings are fully packed, passports are present and correct, what toiletries can be salvaged or chucked, saying goodbye and thanks to the apartment staff. Before we know it, we're on the bus, inevitably hurtling back towards reality.

Sienna is painfully quiet and even I'm struggling for things to say. I'm not sure at this stage what there's left to say.

"Jack asked if I'd swap seats with Kate for the flight so they can sit together," I say eventually. "So you'll have to put up with me a little bit longer." I'm trying to sound light but I feel like there's an edge of resentment creeping in which I can't help. I don't even know why it's there. Do I suddenly feel a bit . . . Used?

Sienna turns to look at me, blue eyes raking my face. "It's hardly been a hardship," she says softly, then her lips curl into a naughty smile. "Well, some things have been hard I suppose."

We both snigger but then silence falls again immediately. She opens her book - my book - and barely speaks again for the rest of the transfer while I think about everything that has happened since I first saw her on the bus a week ago. Never would I have imagined everything that has unfolded between us. I just wish it didn't have to end like this.

We do talk more on the plane though, trying to keep it light. We discuss what we're looking forward to when we get home - she's longing for a long hot bubble bath and I just want to watch some Netflix on my massive TV with a Dominos. I mean, I'd really like to join her in the bath beforehand to be perfectly honest, but I keep that to myself. We've eased from flirty mode down to more of a polite acquaintance small talk level, which is sad but I guess only to be expected.

"Greg messaged me last night." She volunteers as the plane is descending. She's staring straight ahead as she speaks.

"I know," I admit after a brief hesitation. "I saw the message come in."

"He's got a fucking cheek, hasn't he?" she says rhetorically.

"Yeah." I nod emphatically. I don't really feel I can comment much though apart from to back her up. It's not exactly my place.

"Prick," she mutters. That appears to be the end of it. She crosses herself, then holds my arm tightly as we land ("the landing is always the worst part for me" she says), her eyes tightly closed, sitting up ramrod straight in her seat. She slumps in relief as soon as it becomes clear she has survived another flight.

She looks at me and laughs. "We made it."

But we haven't really, I think sadly.

I want to hang on to every little last bit of time I have with her but everything seems to be against me. We disembark quickly, and border control is practically empty when usually the queue snakes around for ages.

Luggage for the flight is already starting to circle the carousel when we emerge from showing our passports.

I'm willing myself to say something, anything, just to put myself out there but it seems I'm just too much of a coward.

"There's my case!" She jumps forward and hauls it onto the ground, not even giving me the option to be a gentleman and get it for her. My heart starts to beat faster as she rummages in her carry-on bag and I know this is it - she's leaving.

"Here." She pulls out her purse and opens it, grabbing a handful of euros and thrusting them into my hand. "For everything you paid for. It doesn't even start to cover it but if you need to hunt me down for more, Kate has my number."

I try to protest but she shakes her head. "Please take it." She meets my eyes briefly and I'm pretty sure I can spot tears in them. "Thanks for everything, Joe. You have no idea how much you've done for me."

With that she stretches up on her tiptoes, cups my face and gives me a sweet but way too short kiss. "Bye Joe," she says softly and then she grabs her case and hurries away.

You know when you're in a dream and you're trying to get somewhere and it's like you're running knee-deep through mud? My reactions are like that right now.

Everything just went too fast for me in the end. I couldn't speak. I barely kissed her back. I watched her get swallowed up by the crowd.

And I didn't say one single thing I wanted to say because I'm a fucking idiot who couldn't just be honest about his feelings. And I can't even chase after her because my case is still missing in action.

I look down at my fists, clenched by my sides, one clutching the money she handed me. I'm smoothing the Euros out, about to put them in my pocket when I realise it's not all money. She's clearly grabbed the notes without paying too much attention and there's a couple of receipts mixed up in there and a small old photograph.

I squint at the photo, holding it away from me so it comes into focus. I realise it's a picture of Sienna when she was younger, maybe mid to late teens, with an older woman who must be her mum judging by the resemblance. True to her words, Sienna had dark hair then; it was a lot longer and falling in wild waves around her cute freckled face. Her eyes look brown in the photo, just like I thought they were when I first saw her on the transfer bus.

And just like I thought they were back . . .

Holy shit. I feel my face slacken in shock.

How the fuck did I not realise sooner?

My case has finally made an appearance so I grab it and hurry out into arrivals, hoping I might catch her.

But she's gone.

Crap.

Chapter 32

Sienna

Coming back to reality after a holiday usually sucks.

Coming back to reality after realising I was harbouring unrequited love for Joe is a whole new level of shit though.

I didn't leave the airport immediately after I ran away from Joe. I hid in a toilet cubicle and cried for about 20 minutes. Then I hid in the pub and cried some more for another hour or so before I finally thought it was safe to get a taxi. Then I cried in the taxi.

I've cried a lot over the past few days.

Gin and "Modern Family" isn't fixing me this time. I've tried wine too. Copious amounts of chocolate. Multiple bubble baths - I had as many as three in one day once. Nothing works.

I haven't seen Kate since the flight. She's still loved up with Jack. We only got back on Wednesday; it's now Monday and she's pretty much been living at his place ever since. So at least it was worth her ditching me, I guess.

How often do holiday romances even turn into more? I wonder. I actually do know a few people who ended up eventually married to folk they met on holiday. It's few and far between though.

I wish it could have worked out for me and Joe.

I know what you're thinking, by the way. You're judging me right now, wondering why I'm acting like there's no way of getting in touch with him.

"Her best friend and his brother are in a relationship now, she could get his number and contact him quite easily, for fucks sake," I can hear you say.

Or "she only lives a couple of streets away from him, hang about long enough and she'll just bloody run into him."

I could do either of these things. I know this. But I'm worried there's no point. Because if he gets bored of me then I'm just back at square one, possibly even more hurt than I already am. Why go chase after him only to end up heartbroken?

Plus it's not like he's been trying to track me down, and maybe that's hurting me too.

I hoped he would realise he couldn't live without me, that I'd find him waiting outside my flat with another bottle of prosecco (I'd even accept flowers I suppose) and make some sort of grand announcement of his everlasting love. That's Dream Scenario A.

Dream Scenario B is slightly lower key: he would just send me a message saying hi, that he missed me. You know, like that message Greg sent me that I didn't even bother to reply to. From Joe, it would mean so much more.

But neither scenario has materialised and I need to accept the fact that he's not interested.

Also to add insult to injury, I'm back at work.

Since the pandemic (mostly) ended, I sometimes work at home and sometimes go into the office. Since me and Greg split up, the office tended to win just so I wasn't alone all the time and, now I'm back from holiday and feeling hopelessly lonely once more, office trumps home again.

It's a good distraction at least, I suppose, getting stuck into my numerous unread emails, trying to establish which tasks I still need to tackle. Going through a version of the same conversation over and over with different colleagues: "yes, I had a great holiday"; "Kefalonia, it's a Greek Island?"; "yeah, it just went way too fast" etc etc.

By mid morning it's like I was never away.

How fucking depressing.

I'm in the kitchen, adding a ginger and lemon teabag to my mug of hot water and half-seriously considering if my employers would let me move to Greece and work remotely, when my best work friend Lindsay appears at my side.

"What's going on?" She asks me bluntly.

"What do you mean?" I play innocent.

"You're not telling me something," she pushes. "I can absolutely read you like a book. What happened on holiday?" Her eyes widen. "Did you . . . Shag someone?"

My blush immediately gives it away.

"Oh my god, tell me everything!" She gasps excitedly.

"There's not that much to tell," I sigh. I prop myself up on a stool at the counter and glance at the TV in the corner. Any further words I was about to say just freeze on my lips as I focus on him.

Joe. Being interviewed on the telly.

I've spent many hours since we parted ways on Google, looking at photos of him, but he still makes me feel swoony. He's clean-shaven today, and he's wearing different glasses - this pair are wire rimmed and might suit him even more than his previous pair. His pale green shirt sets off his tan and brings out the colour of his eyes.

He is totally at ease on camera and utterly gorgeous. And seems absolutely happy and content and experiencing none of the crappy emotions that I am.

I look for the remote to turn the TV up but it is nowhere to be seen and it looks like the segment is coming to an end anyway. Lindsay looks confused at my actions. "Do you know that guy or something?" She asks. She takes another glance at the TV, exhaling a low whistle. "He's hot."

I take a deep breath. "That would be my holiday fling," I announce. And then I burst into tears.

I end up going home early that day, ostensibly to "work from home" but mostly I just end up crying again. The fact Joe was quite clearly not even thinking about me was even more devastating than I thought it might be. I had hoped he might at least have some latent feelings lingering around but I guess that was simply wishful thinking.

I text Kate later that night. Are you free for a couple of drinks one evening this week?x

I want to see her but I also want to see if she knows anything about Joe. I'm a total masochist. A sucker for punishment. I can't help myself.

She takes a few hours to reply. Would Thursday work for you? It's meant to be a nice day - we can sit outside somewhere and pretend we're still on holiday.x

I'd prefer not to have to wait until Thursday but it would be nice to sit in the sun. It's been pretty much raining non-stop since we got back, of course.

I virtually sleep-walk through the next few days. I'm back to the way I was just after Greg, before I went on holiday, almost on auto-pilot.

When Thursday rolls around though, I make an effort. I select the pink dress I last wore on holiday - the night I met Joe, my brain unwillingly reminds me. I can throw a blazer over it for work. I'm excited at the idea of actually going to a pub. I've been so antisocial since I came back. I'm feeling a bit more optimistic - it's amazing the difference sunshine can make to my mindset.

I'm also wondering whether I should ask Kate tonight if she can get Joe's number for me. Maybe I need a bit of closure in order to move on.

Kate has text me to suggest we meet at four at a new pub in the southside. There's a beer garden around the back but because it's new no one really knows the outside bit is there yet. We should get a seat easily.x

I heave a sigh of relief as I leave work and head towards the pub. On my way x I message Kate.

Fab. Come straight through to the back when you get here. A wine is waiting for you x

I push my way into the pub and look for the sign pointing towards the beer garden. The pub itself is relatively empty and the beer garden too only has a handful of people in it. Kate is right.

Kate is also - I realise belatedly - nowhere in sight.

I stop in the doorway and scan the few occupied tables, focusing solely on spotting my best friend. She's definitely not there.

Surely she hasn't stood me up?

My eyes fall on a table directly opposite where I'm standing. There's a glass of white wine - a nice large one, looking very inviting - sitting there without an owner. I track my gaze upwards, towards the proprietor of the pint sitting across from the unclaimed wine.

And that's when I spot him.

Chapter 33

Joe

I've barely stopped thinking about Sienna since she abandoned me at the airport last Wednesday. Even when I'm doing something else - hell, even when I was in the middle of a TV interview the other day - she is always lurking somewhere in the back of my mind.

At first when I couldn't find her in the airport I thought maybe it was for the best. She'd probably had a lucky escape from me. I didn't want to think that way but I'd been so determined that we didn't have a future at first . . . I almost didn't trust my own feelings.

As the days went on though, I'd felt her absence in my life more and more. It wasn't getting easier. And that made me think I needed to take action. I needed to find out if there was a chance, any chance, she was feeling the same as me.

So on Monday evening I swallowed my pride and knocked on my brother's door.

It swung open and Kate was standing there, a knowing expression on her face. She shouted back to Jack "Told you it would be less than seven days."

I eyed her in confusion. "What?"

She laughed. "I said it would be less than a week before you turned up here asking how to get in touch with Sienna. Jack thought it would take longer than that for you to admit it." She grabbed my arm, already acting like she'd been living there for years. "Come on through."

"It's been bloody obvious from the start you were smitten with her," Jack shrugged ten minutes or so later. "I saw the way you were looking at her in the pool bar that first night. It was like you were under a spell and she hadn't even noticed you."

"Rub it in, why don't you," I grumbled, taking a big swig from my bottle of beer. I hadn't realised just how obvious my feelings had been, possibly because I was still in denial myself at that stage. I certainly wouldn't have expected my brother of all folk to pick up on it.

"And don't even get me started on the night we happened to catch you kissing . . . You know, just a few hours after Sienna was adamant nothing was happening between you," Kate laughed. "The chemistry between the two of you could have caused an explosion." She curled up next to Jack, her head resting on his shoulder. "You should know she is absolutely gone for you too."

"She is?" I blinked.

She nodded. "Absolutely. I've known that girl for years, and I could tell she was head over heels. I've never known her to let her guard down with anyone that quickly."

"And you were a different person," Jack added, looking at me. "You've always been so cynical and . . . almost determined to punish yourself, I guess? It's like you allowed yourself to be happy around Sienna."

Once again, I was sort of blown away by my younger brother's level of insight. Had he always been like this?

"So do you want her number?" Kate offered.

That was initially what I was going to ask. But the more I thought about it, the more I wanted to make some sort of gesture. Something to properly show I wanted a relationship with her, that I was willing to invest.

"She messaged me earlier asking me to meet up for a drink this week, but I haven't had a chance to get back to her yet," Kate said slowly when I told them this. "Maybe we employ the old bait and switch method?"

The thought of seeing Sienna again made my heartbeat quicken and at that point I knew I was making the right move.

"And you're sure . . . she would want to see me?" I dared to ask. "I mean, she practically sprinted away from me at the airport."

Kate nodded with certainty. "Look Joe, Sienna has no confidence when it comes to guys. She's been ground down to a pulp by twats like Greg and she thinks she's got nothing to offer. She ran away from you because she thought it was better than you running away from her."

I winced. I couldn't actually imagine actively trying to run away from her any longer. But I couldn't blame her for thinking I might.

And so we put a plan in place. A location. A plan for Kate to meet Sienna there. A couple of texts from Kate to imply she was already at that location, waiting for her.

But instead, I'm here.

And I really hope she's going to want to hear what I have to say . . . And stay.

Chapter 34

Sienna

Joe - or Pool Hotty, or J.P. Quinn, you choose, they're all one and the same - picks up the pint with one hand and takes a sip. As I step forward, his eyes remain on his book but the corners of his lips are gradually curving upwards, and I know he knows I'm there.

My heart slams in my chest.

"Can I sit here?" I ask, doing my best to imitate our original meet-cute.

He puts the book and pint down and raises his head, looking up at me over those sexy wire-rimmed glasses. His eyes are sparkling, crinkling adorably at the corners in that way they do.

"I'm going to say what I should have said then, rather than 'if you must'," he begins, grimacing at the memory of his own words before pausing and gathering himself.

He continues: "I'd love that. I've not been able to stop thinking about you since I first saw you on that bus, and I'm desperate to get to know you better. I'm just not ready to admit that to myself yet."

I can't help but smile at that as I drop into the chair opposite him. "In retrospect, maybe your original response was better. The alternative probably would have been a tad too intense for me and scared me off."

"Agreed." He laughs. "Plus I'm trying to get the conditions as close to our first meeting as possible. Let's see . . ." He screws up his face in thought. "It's Scotland rather than Greece but we've got the sunshine - for a change. It's not a pool bar, but it's a beer garden so it's pretty close. I'm fairly sure you're wearing the same dress but that's just a happy coincidence." He adjusts his glasses higher on his nose, grinning ruefully. "But I'm not even wearing the same specs because I broke my other pair when I was drunk."

"How on earth did you manage to do that?" I ask, giggling.

Joe shrugs, a shadow briefly passing over those chiselled features. "For some reason last Wednesday evening I was feeling really lost, and lonely, and I ended up drinking a bit too much wine and whisky. I left my glasses on the couch and and sat on them. Wish that was a more interesting story but there you have it."

I stare at him, the expression on his face and his words absorbing into my brain as I realise, finally, that this really isn't one-sided. That he's been as miserable as I have at the thought of us not being together. He's just been better at putting a happy face on it.

"So . . . Why are we here?" I ask finally. I pick up the wine and take a sip. Oh goodness, that's refreshing.

"Kate told me chenin is your favourite," Joe sidebars. He pauses again, takes a deep breath, rubbing awkwardly at the scruff already darkening his chin again. "Like I already said, I'm not quite able to make all the conditions work to recreate our first meeting exactly, so forgive me if this doesn't make sense at first . . . But here goes."

It suddenly occurs to me that this isn't Dream Scenario A or B . . . But some sort of scenario is about to unfold and it's going to be a good one. Joe Quinn is about to make a romantic gesture. My insides twist in delight and anticipation at this thought.

He picks up the book he was reading, opens it to the inside back cover and passes it over to me. There is what appears to be a handwritten list scrawled on the blank page at the back, which reminds me of the list we compiled when we agreed to be holiday buddies in the first place.

"For a published author you're terrible for vandalising books," I tut, focusing in on the words. "And you really need to work on your handwriting."

"Just read it," he sighs, pocketing his glasses and running a hand through that messy quiff I love so much. "Well, if it's legible enough."

I start scanning the list in front of me.

"Picnic in the park? Glasgow Mural Trail? Trip to the Science Centre?" Puzzled, I glance up. "What is this?"

Joe looks nervous. "I thought I would put together a list of activities that we could do here in Glasgow. And maybe Scotland in general . . . And maybe outside of Scotland too."

I think I'm finally starting to understand as I return my attention to the list. "Subcrawl? Oh, I've never successfully completed one of those."

"And I've never got around to even trying one," he says hesitantly. "It could be fun?"

"Roadtrip - maybe Skye or the North Coast 500?" I continue to read, trying to contain my excitement as everything starts to become clearer. I really hope I'm not misinterpreting this list's intention.

"Thought we made pretty good roadtrip companions," he nods. "I don't even mind doing all the driving."

"Well, obviously. I have no idea how to work a passing place for a start!" I roll my eyes at him, smiling to soften my words.

I scan down the rest of the list: there's more Glasgow activities on there; there's a trip to the Edinburgh Fringe to watch comedy; a suggestion of another holiday abroad ("but maybe just the two of us this time?"). At the bottom there's one that really stands out for me though.

Rewatch all our favourite sitcoms. At my place, or yours. Doesn't matter as long as we do it together.

I finish reading the list and look up at him, my breathing uneven. My face questioning. My heart brimming with hope.

"So I have a new proposition for you," he says. "But first there's something else I need to tell you." Worry is evident on his face now and the hope is probably draining from mine. My mind is racing; I always think the worst, but I can't even think what the worst case scenario would even be this time.

He pushes something else towards me: a photo. "You accidentally handed me this with the currency," he explains.

I look at the photo of my younger self with my mum. "Told you I look better blonde," I joke. Unable to see where he is going with this.

"Do you remember when you said the girl in my book reminded me of you?" He asks. I nod. He taps the photo.

"It was you. I based Amy on you."

"W-what?" My hands fly to my mouth.

"We had a lecture together. At uni. I didn't make the connection until I saw that photo - like I said before, I've been great at compartmentalising parts of my life - but I changed the whole appearance of Amy after I saw you there. I was drawn to you somehow. The same way I found myself when I met you again two weeks ago." He hesitates. "So, in a weird way, it's always been you."

Oh.

"Hopefully that doesn't freak you out too much," he frowns, looking away.

I can't stop the smile that spreads across my face. "So it turns out the famous author I once had a crush on actually based his female character on me. And now, years later we've reconnected, neither of us realising we sort of had a history? That's pretty cool if you ask me."

Joe exhales, the doubt on his face clearing at my words.

"Can you get on with your proposition now?" I ask eagerly.

He fixes his eyes on me and I find myself, once again, taken back to that day in the pool bar. Less than two weeks ago but it feels like I've known him so much longer. I suppose, in a way, I have.

And suddenly I don't need to have mind-reading abilities to see he feels the same way I do about him. He has fallen too. I bite my lip to stop myself from smiling too soon.

"Sienna," he says softly. "Would you like to be Glasgow buddies?" He swallows hard. "In other words, would you like to continue our holiday buddy agreement here. . . But in a more permanent and definitely less platonic way?"

"We were never very good at being platonic," I nod, trying not to laugh.

"Can we give this a try? Being together? For real?" He finishes.

I repeat the words I did when he propositioned me previously. "Joe, I thought you'd never ask."

His face lights up. We smile at each other, slightly awkwardly, clearly feeling a bit out of our comfort zones. Whatever is going on here is new to both of us. But I'm beyond excited to see where it goes.

"So what happens now?" I ask, after realising we've been gazing into each other's eyes without saying a word for far too long.

Joe stands up and moves around the table to sit beside me. He pulls his new chair up close to me and strokes a finger lightly down my face, brushing his lips against mine softly before he speaks again.

"For a start, in order to continue the recreation of events that started this off, I'm going to take you to the Greek restaurant across the road for dinner. Then . . ." He pauses for dramatic effect. "I'm going to need to go and listen to my brother and your best friend have sex."

I can't help the snort that escapes at that followed by genuine peals of laughter. I'd almost forgotten how much this guy makes me laugh. "Maybe leave that bit out," I manage to say eventually. "How about we skip to the point where I came and rescued you from the lounger and took you back to my room?"

His smile is downright filthy. "Sounds good to me. Except this time I'll act on that little moment we definitely had."

"Not if I beat you to it." I match him dirty grin for dirty grin, wrapping one hand around the back of his neck and pulling his face towards me. He groans, lips sinking onto mine, fingers sliding into my hair.

We kiss for a long time, lost in each other, until eventually someone else in the beer garden eventually breaks the spell by shouting good-naturedly: "Get a room, for fucks sake!"

Typical Glasgow behaviour.

Joe pulls back, looks at me as we both shake with laughter again, the expression in his green eyes a gorgeous mix of tender and horny. "Shall we take their advice?" he asks softly.

"I guess it would be rude not to," I reply breathlessly, as he takes my hand and pulls me to my feet. We head towards the doorway, waving jokingly at our heckler en route.

Holidays are great; they take you away from your normal life, and it's amazing to have that level of escapism . . . but then you've got to go back to reality and the memories quickly fade.

In this case however, I think happily, as Joe bends to kiss me again out on the street, seemingly unable to stop, I've brought back the ultimate souvenir.

A permanent holiday buddy.